RETOLD MYTHS & FOLKTALES

MEXICAN AMERICAN
Folktales

by Esther De Michael Cervantes
and Alex Cervantes

P.S. 94X
3530 Kings College Place
Bronx, NY 10467

D1446643

Perfection Learning®

Writers: Esther De Michael Cervantes and Alex Cervantes
Senior Editor: Terry Ofner
Editor: Shawn Simmons
Cover Photo: iStock Photos
Inside Illustrations: Margaret Sanfilippo
Book Design: Emily Adickes
Reviewers: Robert Franklin Gish, Kata Alvidrez

© 2014 Perfection Learning®
First ebook edition 2014

Please visit our Web site at:
www.perfectionlearning.com

When ordering this book, please specify:

Hardcover (Reinforced Library Edition): ISBN 978-0-7807-7388-2 or **5460302**
Softcover: ISBN 978-0-7891-2397-8 or **5460301**
ebook: ISBN: 978-0-7891-8860-1 or **54603D**

15 16 17 18 19 PP 18 17 16 15 14

All rights reserved. No part of this book may be reproduced, stored in a retrieval
system, or transmitted in any form or by any means, electronic, mechanical,
photocopying, recording, or otherwise, without the prior permission of the
publisher. For information regarding permissions, write to:
Permissions Department, Perfection Learning, 2680 Berkshire Parkway,
Des Moines, Iowa 50325

Printed in the United States of America

ABOUT THE AUTHORS

Esther De Michael Cervantes and Alex Cervantes

Husband and wife team Alex and Esther Cervantes taught upper elementary school in the Los Angeles area for over 20 years. The team has also written stories for children and young adults, including a collection of contemporary ghost stories entitled *Barrio Ghosts* (published by People's Publishing) and short stories in *The Golden Magazine* and *Wee Wisdom Magazine.*

Esther taught journalism for many years in the upper elementary grades. She has also done reporting work for two community newspapers. She enjoys working with kids in drama, art, and writing. But her real love is researching and retelling folktales.

Alex taught at the Carlson Home/Hospital School in the Los Angeles Unified School district. His hobbies include cartooning and devising mystery games for kids. When he's not helping Esther write ghost stories and folktales, you might find Alex going through his extensive comic book collection.

In memory of
Angelo De Michael
and
Cenon Cervantes

TABLE OF CONTENTS

MEXICAN
AMERICAN
Folktales

I remember entering a bakery in East Los Angeles as a child and seeing a striking picture of two lovers on a calendar—a prince carried a princess in his arms. I was impressed by the beauty of the illustration, but I knew nothing about its background. It wasn't until years later that I heard the story of Izta and Popo and came to understand the significance of the image. Folktales are like that. They are all around us. We encounter them even before reading them, or hearing them told.

Alex, my husband and coauthor, remembers his own early encounters with Mexican folktales. He was born and raised in a barrio in San Gabriel, California. On Saturday afternoons, he often walked to the movies with his brother and sister, and on the way home, they talked about La Llorona, the weeping woman. "Usually it was dark," he says, "and we would imagine La Llorona following us. La Llorona was hiding out there, we believed. 'Where are my children, Oooooo!' we'd shriek. The stories were very much a part of our lives."

Since those early encounters, Alex and I have read many folktales. We both love the ghost stories of Mexico and the Southwest. They are filled with imagination and wonder. I first heard about the ghostly figure, La Llorona, while teaching. Students told me stories about La Llorona chasing them home from basketball practice when they stayed too late. Through research, I discovered many versions of her story and became fascinated by it and other legends.

Our research for this collection of stories was an adventure. We discovered both new versions of familiar stories and stories that were entirely new to us. Alex was surprised to find the Dos Compadres stories and the coyote trickster tales. Even though he's Mexican American and enjoys telling folktales to his students, he wasn't familiar with these wonderful, funny tales.

We hope you enjoy reading these tales as much as we've enjoyed discovering and retelling them. In addition, we hope you share them with your family and friends and—someday— your own children.

RETOLD UPDATE

This book presents a collection of eight adapted stories from Mexico and the Southwestern United States. The regions of Mexico and the Southwestern United States have been inhabited by Spanish-speaking people for centuries. Until the Mexican American War of 1848, Mexico occupied most of the Southwest.

When the United States acquired the Southwestern states, most of the Spanish-speaking people living there became U.S. citizens. Settlers from the Eastern United States poured into the area and soon outnumbered the Mexican Americans in every area except New Mexico.

In this collection, a word list has been added at the beginning of each story. Each word defined on the list is printed in dark type within the story. If you forget the meaning of one of these words, just check the list to review the definition.

You'll also find footnotes at the bottom of some story pages. These notes identify people or places, explain ideas, show pronunciations, or provide cultural information.

You will also find more cultural information in the Insights section after each tale. These revealing facts will add to your understanding of Mexican Americans.

One last word. Since many of these stories have been handed down for centuries, several versions exist. So a story you read here will probably differ from a version you read elsewhere.

Now on to the folktales. We hope you discover the mystery and adventure of these Mexican American stories.

Map of the
Southwestern United States
and Mexico

GHOSTS AND HAUNTINGS

Voice in the Wind

The Soldier and the Ghost

Ghosts and spirits appear in many Mexican American stories. They rarely appear as terrifying ghouls or goblins. Instead they are the souls of people who have returned from the dead, usually to settle a matter.

The ghosts in Mexican American tales come back to earth for a short period. A few come back for revenge. Most come back to set right an error or to give advice. Notice the way the ghosts in the following tales treat those that they encounter.

Voice in the Wind

VOCABULARY PREVIEW

The following words appear in the story. Review the list and get to know the words before you start the story.

betrayed—proven false; let down
bewildered—confused; puzzled
burden—heavy load; hardship
descended—moved downward; alighted
disown—abandon; reject
dissolved—vanished; faded away
eerie—strange; weird
glared—stared angrily; scowled
grieve—cry; feel sad
luminous—glowing; full of light
mournful—sad; sorrowful
nestled—settled comfortably
predicted—foretold; prophesied
sapphire—deep purplish blue
vain—proud; conceited

MAIN CHARACTERS

María—a beautiful girl
José Luís—a young man who is in love with María
Antonio—wealthy ranchero's son

Voice in the Wind

*In the night, a woman weeps
for her lost children.
Her sorrow rides an icy wind.*

It was a warm, clear night in the *barrio*.[1] A white-haired man sat on a porch swing watching his niece play in the front yard. The man sipped an *horchata*[2] and looked up at the deep blue-black California sky.

Down by the lake, a reflection of the moon shone on the water. Clouds drifted across the moon, and the sound of far-off thunder drummed across the heavens.

The girl stopped playing and listened as the sound of soft crying echoed through the shadows. Lightning crackled, turning the night an **eerie** white. Suddenly the wind picked up. Then a voice rushed past on the chilly air.

"*Tío*,[3] what was that?" the girl asked.

"I don't know," her uncle replied. "Look!" He pointed to the crossroads near the house. A shape in a long white gown glided along the street. The dim figure seemed to float a few feet above the pavement. The thin layers of her dress rustled like dead leaves. Her **mournful** words pierced the night.

"Ohhh! Why did you betray me, my love?" moaned the figure. "Ohhh! *Mis niños*,[4] where have I sent you? Where have you gone, my children?"

A shiver ran through the girl. "Who is that woman?" she whispered. "Why is she crying?"

"It's the sad, lonely woman," her uncle replied. "My grandmother called her *La Llorona*.[5] I first heard her story when I was a little boy growing up in Southern California."

---

1   (VAH rreoh) A *barrio* is a neighborhood.
2   (ohr CHA tah) An *horchata* is a beverage made of water and ice and flavored with almonds or orange flowers.
3   (TEE oh) *Tío* means "uncle."
4   (Mees Nee nyohs) The phrase *mis niños* means "my children."
5   (Lah Yoh ROH nah) *La Llorona* means "the woman who weeps."

* * *

A long time ago, in the days of the ranches, there lived a proud and beautiful girl named María. When she was little, everyone told María that someday she'd break many hearts. And she did. By the time she was sixteen, young men from miles around the ranch had fallen in love with her. María's black hair was straight and hung below her small waist. Her skin was **luminous** and the color of honey. Her eyes were large, full-lidded, and dark—so dark.

Of all the young men, José Luís was most in love with María. He knew she was proud and **vain.** But he loved her. He loved her beauty, her strengths, and even her weaknesses. José Luís tried to win María's heart by bringing her roses and other gifts. Her favorite was a gold locket in the shape of a heart. She wore it always, but she didn't want to marry José Luís.

"Why don't you marry that young man?" her grandmother asked. "He's thoughtful and good-hearted. He'd make a wonderful husband."

"I know he would, Grandmother." María thought of his eyes—his smile. "José Luís is handsome and generous. But he's poor. When I get married, I want a handsome man—but he'll have to be rich too."

"Wealth and good looks aren't everything, María. It's wiser to marry a kind man who loves you and who will take care of you and your children."

María laughed. "Oh, Grandmother. That's why you're so poor. I'm not going to live in a *casita*[6] forever. I want to live in a *hacienda*[7] and wear beautiful clothes. I'll go to all the *fiestas*[8] and dances. We'll have parties all the time. That's how I want to live."

The next evening, there was a party at the ranch. María wore her best dress—a long blue gown with layers of petticoats. She wore flowers in her braided hair. At her throat **nestled** the heart-shaped locket from José Luís.

---

6   (Kah SEE tah) A *casita* is a small house.
7   (ah see END dah) An *hacienda* is a ranch.
8   (FEE EHS tahs) *Fiestas* are festivals or parties.

María knew that Antonio, the wealthy rancher's son, would be there. She was ready for him. She danced, she smiled, she dazzled, she enchanted. When she caught Antonio's eye, he smiled. María smiled back.

The rancher's son walked toward her. María's heart beat fast. Everyone's eyes were on her. Everyone watched to see what would happen next.

"Would you like to dance?" Antonio asked.

"Yes, I would," María answered, a laugh in her voice.

María and Antonio danced in dizzying circles around the glittering room. They talked, they ate, they strolled through the moonlit garden. They danced again and then again.

"We're made for each other," Antonio whispered.

"Yes. This was meant to be," she told him.

After that night, they were always together. María's heart was won, and she was happy. But her grandmother saw trouble ahead.

"This man will break your heart, María."

"Oh, Grandmother. Antonio loves me. Nothing can come between us."

Grandmother shook her head. "His family will come between you. They want their son to marry a girl from a wealthy family—a girl brought up to be the wife of a rancher."

María held her head high. "I can do that. I can weave, cook . . . ."

"He needs a wife to run the ranch, María. To order supplies, plan meals for the workers, keep everything comfortable for him and his family."

"Oh, Grandmother—people always tell me I'm smart. Surely I'll learn how to do all of those things."

Grandmother looked into her granddaughter's eyes. "Listen to me, María. Antonio's parents know how to get their way. They will take away his money. **Disown** him."

María laughed. "They wouldn't do that, Grandmother. He's their son."

Grandmother sighed. "You're young. You don't know how cruel people can be. And you really don't know Antonio either.

He's wild, María. He's been engaged to other girls. He broke their hearts. He'll break yours too."

María turned away. "You're wrong, Grandmother. He loves only me. And I love him."

Not long after, in the little church in town, María and Antonio were married.

Time passed and María had twin boys. Her husband and children were everything to her. And, for a time, she was happy. Then Antonio grew impatient with her. Sometimes he stayed out late. Soon there were no more or *fiestas*. There were no moonlight walks beneath the California sky. He stopped buying her gifts. Then one day María realized that her husband no longer called her beautiful.

"Why do you come home so late?" she asked one night.

"I'm working."

"But your *niños*[9] miss you. They ask me why you're not here with them—and me."

He **glared** at her with anger in his eyes. "This town and everyone in it bore me. I don't want to live like a *peón*.[10] I need money, a good horse, and freedom. You and your precious twins are a **burden** to me."

María's heart stopped. She reached for her locket. "You don't want me or the children. You don't care about us."

Antonio didn't answer. But María knew. And like a ghost, Grandmother's words came back to her. " . . . Marry a kind man who loves you and who will take care of you and the children."

The next evening, Antonio didn't come home. When he did return, he hardly spoke to María. He began staying away for days at a time. María didn't know what to do. She wept every day. One day she even forgot to feed the twins. They began to cry because they were hungry and scared and because their mother was so sad.

"Don't cry, my sweet *gemelos*,"[11] she told them. "Spring will be here soon. Everything will be better when spring comes."

---

9   (NEE nyohs) *Niños* means "children."

10   (peh OHN) A *peón* is a poor person.

11   (heh MEH lohs) *Gemelos* means "twins."

One fine spring day when the sun shone out of a deep blue sky and the fields burst with flowers, Antonio rode up to María's *casita* in a fine carriage. On the seat beside him sat a richly dressed young woman.

María glanced at her own faded dress and dusty shoes. She brushed back a strand of hair and watched as Antonio **descended** from the carriage. He carried several boxes to the porch.

"Papi! Papi!" the twins cried as they ran to him.

"I can't stay, my sons," he told them. "But I brought food and gifts."

Then, without speaking to his wife, Antonio turned away and strode back to the carriage. He jumped to the seat and yelled to his horses. The carriage rolled forward. How could he ride away without saying anything? Was he just going to ride off with his carriage wheels blowing dust around her?

"My husband!" María cried. "Where are you going? What are you doing to us?"

Antonio pulled the carriage to a stop. "I tried, María. But I can't stay with you. I'm going up North."

María held her head high. "Who is that woman?"

"She's the woman I love," he replied. "We're engaged."

"How can you marry her when you're married to me?" María demanded.

"It's over, María."

María looked at the woman in the carriage. Her many jewels and fine clothes could not disguise her plain features. "She is not beautiful, Antonio," María said.

She looked at the woman, who met her gaze without expression. "He will leave you too," María **predicted.**

Antonio put one arm around the woman. "Good-bye, María."

"How do you expect us to live? Who will take care of us, Antonio?"

"Go back to your family," he replied. "Go back to your own people."

María watched the couple ride away. She watched until all she could see was a trail of dust. She couldn't go back to her family. Grandmother was dead, and her other relatives lived far away. She couldn't—wouldn't—live with them anyway. Everyone would know that Antonio had left her. How could she face them? How could she face anyone here?

"Ohhh! What will become of us? What shall I do? Where can we go?"

María cried all that day. Then her tears turned to screams of rage. She didn't eat. She couldn't sleep. The twins had never seen their mother like this. They were scared and **bewildered.**

"Mamita, what's wrong?"

"Mamita, why did Papi go away?"

María stopped crying and looked at her children. "They're so innocent," she thought, "so beautiful." She tried to smile.

"Papi's gone, my little ones. But I'll be here, always. I'll never leave you, I promise."

The twins stared at their mother and began to cry. They clung to each other for comfort.

"Oh, stop your crying now." María brushed away their tears and smiled. "Everything will be all right. Let's walk through the field and pick some flowers. Then we'll go to the lake."

She took each twin by the hand. Together they walked down the path leading to the field. They picked baskets of flowers and chased butterflies. Then they walked to the lakeside. "You can help me carry the laundry basket."

The three stood at the edge of the water. María watched its sparkling surface as it reflected the **sapphire** sky. Except for the gentle sounds of the water, all was quiet. "Stay near me while I wash clothes," Maria told the twins.

As she worked María remembered the happy days with her grandmother. "If only I had listened to her. José Luís cared for me. If only . . ."

"¡Mamita! Help!"

Maria looked up. Somehow the twins had wandered into the water. They were struggling to keep their heads above water.

"My children!" she screamed.

She watched as the waves pulled the twins until their little round faces went under and María couldn't see them anymore. They were gone. Lost forever.

María ran fast along the edge of the lake. "Ohhh! My children—Where are you?" she cried. "Come back, niños. Ohhh I can't lose you. I can't leave you here. I must find you."

She leaped into the water. She didn't struggle. She let the water pull her down; she let the water take her under.

The next morning, a townsperson found María's body on the shore. The twins were never recovered. The townspeople buried María near the lake.

That should have been the end of this story of love **betrayed.** But María's story has no ending.

On the evening of María's funeral, José Luís brought roses to her grave. He wept as he covered her tombstone with flowers.

A full moon, pale as a ghost, shone in the blue-black sky, and the stars glittered like pieces of ice. A sudden gust of wind rippled the water, and a sigh breathed through the shadows. José Luís heard a rustling like dead leaves and turned. He caught his breath and stared.

María stood before him, smiling her enchanting smile. He recognized her but couldn't speak. She was so beautiful. He had loved María when they were young, and now he knew he would love her always.

She wore the dress he loved best—the same dress she had worn the night she met Antonio. But now the blue dress was white and luminous like the moon. And its thin layers of fabric rustled like the sound of fallen leaves.

María's eyes shone with tears. José Luís found her beautiful even when she cried. Her hair was long and unbraided. And she wore his heart-shaped locket around her pale neck.

In a hollow voice that rushed out on the wind, María asked, "Do you love me still, José Luís?"

"Yes, María. You know I do."

She was silent. Tears glistened on her face. She moaned, and the wind shook the leaves from the trees.

"Don't **grieve** so, María. It breaks my heart."

She looked at him with sad, longing eyes. "Have you forgiven me for hurting you, José Luís?"

"Long ago, María. Long ago."

She glided sideways in front of him. Then she pulled—or was pulled—away, her arms outstretched to him. She floated across the water, the hem of her gown trailing in the lake. Slowly she was swept to the middle of the lake where she **dissolved** into a mist.

José Luís returned often to her grave, but he never saw her ghost again.

Many others believe they've seen her spirit and heard her crying. But people no longer know her as María. They call her La Llorona, the woman who weeps. Some say she has a beautiful face. Others say her face is hidden by her long hair. Still others say that when she floats past them her face looks like a skull and the wind that carries her is like ice.

*   *   *   *

"That cry we heard tonight," said the man to his niece, "was it only the wind in the trees? Was the white shape we saw gliding along the path La Llorona—or just a trick of the moon and the shadows?"

"I don't know, *Tío,* but it looked so real."

"My grandmother would say that we have heard the voice in the wind, the voice of La Llorona. We have heard her weeping and crying for her children."

INSIGHTS

Who is La Llorona? And why does she walk along the river banks and haunt lakes? Why does she weep and mourn and walk the lonely paths in the night? And why do people fear her?

Some believe the legend of La Llorona began when the goddesses called Cihuapipíltin died while giving birth. These goddesses come back to earth to hurt people. They are believed to steal infants from their cradles and to bring about convulsions. Wise travelers sometimes leave offerings at crossroads where the goddesses are believed to hide in the shadows.

Others say La Llorona is the goddess Cihuacóhuatl. Her twins were sacrificed to the gods. And now, dressed in a long white robe, she is seen at night, mourning and weeping. The goddess carries an empty cradle on her shoulders and searches cities for her lost children. She usually disappears after reaching a lake or river.

Still others believe La Llorona is the ghost of Marina, an Indian who was a translator and companion of Hernán Cortés. Marina fell in love with Cortés and helped the Spaniard conquer Mexico. According to legend, Marina bore a child to Cortés, and shortly afterward she was replaced by a highborn Spanish wife. Her jealousy led her to strike out against the Spaniards.

The more common stories of La Llorona are simple ones of love betrayed. In one version, María tries to gain entry into heaven after killing her children and herself, but the Lord refuses her entry. The Lord then asks her, "Where are your children?" Ashamed, she lies and tells Him she doesn't know. The Lord replies by telling her that she cannot rest until they are found.

Since this encounter with the Lord, La Llorona wanders near streams at night, crying for her children. She usually dresses in white, and her face looks horribly blank. According to some, she has been known to take revenge on men she encounters at night.

The story of La Llorona is often told as an obedience tale. Parents tell it to their children to warn them about staying out late at night. The story is also frequently used to warn teenage girls about falling in love with a man who is too far above them for marriage.

The Soldier and the Ghost

VOCABULARY PREVIEW

The following words appear in the story. Review the list and get to know the words before you read the story.

bodice—fitted waist of a dress
dreary—gloomy; bleak
enchanting—charming; intriguing
lashed—whipped; beat
lulling—calming; soothing
mingled—mixed; combined
murmured—spoke softly; muttered
quickened—sped up; accelerated
resurrect—revive; restore
reverie—daydreaming; musing
sloshed—splashed
smacked—slapped; struck
transparent—clear; see-through

MAIN CHARACTERS

Johnny—a soldier who has recently returned from war
Alma—a young woman

Our sweet angel
Our daughter

Born
Died

The Soldier and the Ghost

Adapted from a tale set in Southern California

*Alma seems mysterious when Johnny meets
her on the Macy Street Bridge.
She is beautiful, and she understands him so
well. But why is she unsure of her past?
And why is she afraid to go home?*

On a bleak November night in 1945, Johnny drove his black Chevy along Brooklyn Avenue in East Los Angeles. The sky was black, and an icy wind blew through the pines and palms. Johnny watched as rain droplets, like a sparkling necklace, beaded across the windshield.

Johnny didn't mind the **dreary** weather. He was home. Home at last. And the war—that long, long nightmare—was finally over. Johnny wanted to **resurrect** his old life. In the days before the war, he liked going to dances. He knew all the latest songs and dance steps.

He wanted to enjoy life again. And dancing, more than anything, made him feel alive. Dancing made him forget the war, forget the loneliness and losses of the last four years.

Johnny drove along Brooklyn until it became Macy Street, just before the bridge that led into Los Angeles. He couldn't wait to get to El Palacio.[1] He might meet someone there, someone who liked music and dancing as much as he did. It would be nice to have a girlfriend.

---

1   (Ehl   pah LAH seeoh) El Palacio, which means "The Palace," is a dance hall.

A shadow moved along the bridge and vanished.

"What was that?" Johnny asked out loud. He slowed down and peered into the mist. Huge raindrops splattered against the windshield. Johnny turned on the windshield wipers.

Wook-whoosh, wook-whoosh, they went. A comforting sound. Johnny saw a girl hurrying across the bridge. He drove the Chevy alongside the curb. The girl turned to look at him as Johnny rolled down the window.

"Do you need a ride?" he asked. "It's going to start pouring soon."

The girl smiled. "Oh, yes. It's so cold out here." She opened the door and carefully stepped into the car.

Johnny glanced at her. No coat or umbrella. Just a party dress and satin shoes with narrow straps over the instep. Dancing shoes.

"Where are you going on such a stormy night?" he asked.

"Dancing. I love to dance." Her voice was like music. "So, where are you going tonight, soldier?"

"El Palacio."

"Oh, yes. That's a beautiful ballroom. I haven't been there in a long time."

"Would you like to go there tonight?"

She turned to him, her eyes shining. "*Me encantaría,*[2] I would love to."

Johnny drove along the bridge. He turned on the radio. The song "Button Up Your Overcoat" played while gentle rain pattered on the car roof. The angel-like girl beside him **quickened** his heartbeat. Her hair, black and satin-smooth, was cut short in the back and longer in the front with bangs to frame her perfect face. Her eyes were large, and though she smiled, there was a sadness in them. He wondered why she was sad. Was it possible that such a beautiful young woman could be lonely just like him?

A tunnel loomed ahead. It would be lit up inside, and the shining tiles along the walls would reflect the cars racing through. Johnny turned off the radio when the song was replaced with static.

---

2   (meh   ehn KAHN tah REE ah) *Me encantaría* means "I'd love to."

"Oh, look! The tunnel," exclaimed the girl. "I haven't gone through it in so long. Honk the horn, soldier."

Johnny beeped the horn and then held it down as they shot through the long tunnel. Other drivers honked too.

"I love L.A." She laughed. "Don't you love the city, especially at night?"

"Yes. I really missed it a lot. It's great being home again."

He turned on the windshield wipers. The rain fell harder, and the friendly patter on the roof turned to pelting. Blinding rain **smacked** against the windshield. Layers of rain fell against the long hood of the Chevy. Swirling rain **lashed** the sides of the car.

Johnny glanced at the girl, who looked almost gray in the shadows of rain and car. She stared straight ahead, and when Johnny talked, she didn't move or speak.

"Are you all right, miss?"

She sighed. "I don't like storms. The thunder scares me."

"Thunder's harmless," he told her. "It's the lightning that's dangerous."

The girl turned to him, fear in her eyes. "It's strange how it lights up everything, even in the darkest parts of the night. And you can see things you're not supposed to see—things you don't want to see."

Johnny frowned. "What do you mean?"

She shrugged. "Oh, let's not talk about that any more." She took a comb from her small beaded purse. She combed down her bangs and the sides of her hair. "Let's talk about you, soldier. Where have you been traveling? Europe, I imagine. It must have been really hard, the war and all."

Johnny turned away and stared out at the rain. He followed a truck whose wheels threw out arcs of spray. Johnny remembered another night when rain flooded narrow streets, turning them into rivers of mud. He remembered the tanks in front of him as he **sloshed** through the mud. The tanks boomed into the thundering night. And he remembered the screams of people unseen in the blinding storm and darkness.

He wanted to forget that night and many other nights. He wanted to leave it behind, to bury it forever. Johnny turned the steering wheel to the left and shot around the truck. Rain fell over the Chevy, and the girl gasped as they sped ahead, leaving the truck far behind.

Johnny looked at the girl. She was afraid of the storm, and now she might be afraid of him too. He saw her shiver.

"There's a car blanket on the back seat, miss."

She reached for the blanket. "I've got it. This will help a lot."

Johnny smiled at her, and she smiled back. She was beautiful, even wrapped in an old car blanket. He turned on the radio. "What's your name?"

"Alma. What's your name, soldier?"

"Juanito,[3] but everyone calls me Johnny."

"Johnny," she repeated. "I like that name."

The sad, sweet lyrics of "Body and Soul" played as Johnny drove down Spring Street. The rain slowed to a gentle, steady rhythm.

*   *   *

El Palacio with its rainbows of turning lights and stardust ceiling hadn't changed. Johnny couldn't believe he was there. And Alma was **enchanting.** She was an old-fashioned girl in a dress that reminded him of the 1930s. Her dress was autumn gold trimmed with black beads—like necklaces—on the **bodice** and down the center of the long skirt.

The band began playing, and Johnny led Alma to the dance floor. He began jitterbugging. Alma couldn't keep up with him.

"Oh, the music is so fast," she told him, "and the steps are new."

Alma didn't know which way to go when Johnny tried to swing her. She didn't know any of the steps or how to turn. Johnny slowed down and showed her the steps.

"What is this dance called?" she asked.

"The jitterbug."

"What a funny word. *¿Cómo se díce?*"[4]

---

3   (Wah NEE toh) The name *Juanito* is "Johnny" in Spanish.
4   (KOH moh seh dee seh) *¿Cómo se díce?* means "How do you say it?"

"Jitterbug."

"Jitterbug." She laughed. "It's so crazy, such a *loco*[5] dance. I like it, though."

Alma caught on fast. But after awhile she got tired and wanted to rest. They sat at their table. Alma sipped a Shirley Temple,[6] and Johnny drank a Coca-Cola out of the frosty green bottle.

"It's been such a long time," she told Johnny. "I don't know any of the songs."

"They're playing lots of new songs tonight," Johnny said. "Most of them are new to me too."

"Listen! *¡Escucha!*[7] Oh, Johnny, I remember this song. It's one of my favorites."

"Let's dance then."

They waltzed to "Falling in Love with Love," and the lyrics went round and round in Johnny's head. They danced to "Got a Date with an Angel" and "Heart and Soul."

Then the band played Latin music: the *rumba,* the *samba,* and the *mambo.* And Alma was unbelievable. Every step Johnny knew, she knew too. She could even dance to "Begin the Beguine," which was tropical music and a lot different from the other Latin dances that Johnny knew.

"Oh, Johnny—they're playing '*Solamente una vez*'—one of my favorites."

She sighed and leaned against Johnny as they danced. She felt cool, and he breathed in her perfume.

* * *

It was still raining when they left El Palacio. But they didn't mind the rain. They laughed and sang "I've Got My Love to Keep Me Warm" as they walked to Johnny's car.

Johnny turned on the radio, and Alma listened as he sang "And the Angels Sing."

---

5 (LOH koh) *Loco* means "crazy."
6 A *Shirley Temple* is a nonalcoholic drink made from soda and grenadine, a syrup flavored with pomegranates.
7 (Ehs KOO cha) *¡Escucha!* means "Listen!"

The rain was soft, **lulling.** Johnny drove on until he reached the bridge on Macy Street. "Where do you live, Alma?"

She hesitated. "Oh, you can just drop me off on the bridge."

"I don't want to leave you all alone so late at night and in this rain. Let me drive you home. It isn't safe here."

"Safe?" Alma looked out at the bridge. "Safe?" she repeated, looking up at Johnny.

Her eyes—why did she look so sad? "What's wrong Alma?"

She looked out her side window. "It was raining the last time I went out. I remember it was a while back. Maybe a long while back."

Alma took a small lace-edged handkerchief out of her purse. She looked at Johnny, and he noticed how deep-set her eyes were at that moment.

"What were you doing out alone tonight?"

"I needed—I wanted to go dancing. That's the only thing that makes me feel happy and—alive."

Alma twisted the little handkerchief. Her hands—so beautiful; the skin, almost **transparent.**

"I—I don't remember how I got to the bridge, Johnny."

"You don't remember?"

"No. I was just there."

Johnny wondered why she was lying. She must be lying. But why?

"But I can't—I won't leave you here, Alma. I want to take you home."

"Oh, Johnny, I can't go home tonight. I can't ever go home again."

Johnny stared out at the empty street. The rain was silent but still falling, a fine mist turned pale gold by city lights.

"Why can't you go home, Alma? Is your family angry with you?"

She shook her head. "No. It's nothing like that. I'm very close to them."

"Then let me take you home. We'll go up to the front door and knock. Someone will answer, and everything will be fine."

"I've already tried to go home, Johnny. I knock at the door, but nobody answers. So I knock again—I even bang on the door and beg them to come. I—I don't think they can hear me." She was silent for a moment. Then she said, "Sometimes, I feel lost. The world is changing, and I can't keep up with everything. Sometimes, I forget things."

Gently, Johnny told her, "Don't worry. Everything will be okay. Do you remember where you live?"

"In a little white house on Eastern Avenue."

Johnny smiled. "We'll go there now."

Lightning streaked through the sky, and thunder cracked again. Alma shivered. Johnny reached over and touched her hands. A strange chill swept through him. He was afraid, afraid for her.

"Your hands are like ice, Alma. My poor angel." He draped the car blanket around her.

Alma smiled. "I like when you call me that, Angel. It makes me feel loved again."

Her house was in shadows from the tall trees and bushes. Johnny wanted to walk her to the door, but she insisted on going alone. She turned and looked at him with sad eyes.

"I'll never forget you, Johnny. *Adiós, mi amor.*"[8]

He waited near the fence as she opened the little gate and walked up the stone pathway. She was so graceful when she moved. She seemed to float up the porch steps. He heard a rapping sound and watched. Shifting shadows surrounded her, and Johnny moved closer to the gate. He thought he saw candlelight from inside the house.

"Where is she?" he asked aloud. He walked halfway up the path. He saw the whole porch now. She was gone.

Johnny walked back to the Chevy. He waited inside the car for a few minutes, hoping Alma would wave from one of the windows. But she didn't. He started the Chevy and drove home.

Johnny was already home when he remembered she took the car blanket. And there, on the front seat of the car, lay her gold scarf with the black trim. Johnny held the scarf to his face and closed his eyes.

Later that night, Johnny lay awake and thought of Alma. The rain, the comforting, gentle rain, lulled him into **reverie.**

8   (Ah DEEOHS, mee ah MOHR) *Adiós, mi amor* means "Good-bye, my love."

He turned on his phonograph and listened to "I'll Never Smile Again." The soulful notes **mingled** with the rain. He looked out his window at the shimmer of rain. He couldn't stop thinking of Alma. Like music, memories of her played and replayed in his mind all through the night.

*   *   *

In the morning, Johnny dressed and hurried through breakfast. Then he drove to Alma's house. He opened the little gate and walked up the path. He skipped steps running up to the porch. He knocked and waited.

A tired-looking man answered the door.

"Good morning. I'm here to see Alma. We went dancing last night."

The man stared at Johnny. "I'm sorry, soldier. Alma's not here."

"Oh. May I come back later? She left her scarf in my car."

The man took the scarf. "I know, son. But you see, Alma, our sweet daughter, died five years ago."

Johnny was stunned. "There must be some mistake, sir. I danced with her, talked to her. I drove her home to this house last night."

The man opened the door wide. "Come in, soldier."

Johnny stepped inside. A woman with eyes like Alma's smiled at him. "Please come to the dining room." She showed Johnny an altar with a photograph of Alma.

"That's Alma, the girl I danced with last night."

Johnny stared at the altar. On top of it lay a Shirley Temple with melting ice, *pan de muertos*,[9] tamales, *buñuelos,*[10] and a beaded purse—like the one Alma carried last night. Two bouquets of marigolds decorated the table. And paper streamers of monarch butterflies framed the photograph of Alma.

"I don't understand," Johnny **murmured.** "This is an offering. Tell me it isn't true."

---

9   (pahn deh MWEHR tohs) *Pan de muertos* means "bread of the dead."

10   (voo NWEH los) *Buñuelos* are pastries sprinkled with powdered sugar.

Alma's father spread the scarf along the edge of the table. "Each year on *El día de los muertos*, [11] Alma's spirit comes home. Today would be her birthday. She was killed in an automobile accident on Macy Street—on the bridge. She's buried in Calvary Cemetery. Do you know where that is, soldier?"

*   *   *

Johnny drove to Calvary. He found the tombstone, the one guarded by the statue of an angel. He forced himself to look at the grave. Then he covered his face and wept.

Our daughter, ALMA
Our sweet angel
Born November 2, 1918
Died October 24, 1940

Neatly folded on top of the grave was the car blanket, covered with raindrops that sparkled in the morning sun.

INSIGHTS

"The Soldier and the Ghost" is one of the vanishing hitchhiker stories, a group of tales widely told in the Southwestern United States. In these tales, a person, usually a woman, appears mysteriously and seeks a ride from a stranger. The woman tells the driver her destination, and either before or after reaching it, she disappears and leaves the driver baffled.

Variations on the hitchhiker story are endless. In one version of "The Soldier and the Ghost," a boy picks up a girl and takes her to a dance. He lends the girl his jacket. The next day, the boy goes to the girl's house to get his jacket and learns she's been dead for ten years. The boy and the girl's mother then go to the cemetery and find the jacket draped over the girl's tombstone.

Most of the vanishing hitchhiker tales exist through oral tradition only. A few of the most intriguing have been collected and written down. In the early 1930s, newspapers occasionally

---

11   (ehl DEE ah deh lohs MWehr tohs) *El día de los muertos* is the Day of the Dead, a Mexican holiday.

printed the stories. One of the most memorable hitchhiking tales is about a man and his son who pick up a hitchhiker on the way back to their ranch.

The man and his son stop to pick up the woman and realize immediately something isn't right. The man asks her where she is going. She answers, "I'm going where you're going." And so the man reluctantly takes her to the ranch. While she is there, she spots a porch swing and sits down. Later that evening, the man tells her that it is getting late and that he is going to sleep. When he doesn't hear any response, he walks closer to the swing, looks down, and sees only a doll.

The character Alma, whose name means "soul" in Spanish, is typical of ghostly figures found in Mexican American literature. She is lifelike in appearance and returns to Earth with a purpose in mind. Her spirit visits each year around the Days of the Dead, a Mexican holiday celebrated November first and second. Her parents prepare for her visit with an offering.

Alma is dressed in golden orange and black to represent the monarch butterfly. The monarchs return to Mexico around the Days of the Dead. It is believed that the butterflies bear the spirits of loved ones on their gossamer wings. The insects fly in densely packed lines and look like orange and black streamers.

The bridge on Macy Street still exists today. A plaque on each side of the bridge dedicates it to Father Junípero Serra (1713–1784). If Johnny had lived at the time of Father Serra, he might have been a soldier from Mexico. He would have resided at one of the many *presidios*, or forts, which were used to protect the missions. He would have been called by his Spanish name, Juan or Juanito.

TRICKSTERS

The Adventures of Ovejita and Señor Coyote

The Badger and the Rattlesnake

Tricksters have amused readers in tales throughout the world. They are mischievous creatures who often cause big trouble.

Several tricksters appear in Mexican American stories. The most well known is Señor Coyote. An unpredictable creature, he is sometimes clever and other times gullible. Often he calls another creature his friend and then turns around and makes him into a meal.

Mexican American trickster tales are often humorous. But important lessons can be found in the foolish actions of characters like Señor Coyote.

The Adventures of Ovejita and Señor Coyote

VOCABULARY PREVIEW

The following words appear in the story. Review the list and get to know the words before you read the story.

braced—placed firmly (against)
churning—agitated; moving violently
cunning—sly; clever
elusive—mysterious; hard to grasp
fleece—the wool covering of a sheep
forlorn—miserable; hopeless
glinted—glimmered; sparkled
lagoon—lake; a shallow pond near a larger body of water
profusion—abundance
repertoire—collection; list
scampered—ran away
sheared—cut; clipped
shimmering—glistening; shining
sprigs—small branches

MAIN CHARACTERS

Ovejita—a small sheep
Señor Coyote—a clever coyote

The Adventures of Ovejita and Señor Coyote

Tales set in Texas

The sheepherders from Mexico and the
Southwest tell many stories about
Señor Coyote, a cunning creature who is
usually into mischief. In the following tale, he
encounters a brave sheep named Ovejita.

The Moon Is a Big Round Cheese

Ovejita[1] lived on a ranch near a meadow in Texas. She loved her home on the hillside with its mesquite[2] trees, bluebonnets, and tender *zacate*.[3] Ovejita looked forward to the endless blue Texas skies. And she felt at peace when she thought about the clear Texas nights shimmering and twinkling with countless stars.

One spring day, Ovejita sat under a *mesquite* tree at the edge of the meadow. Feeling safe and happy, Ovejita began grazing on sweet *zacate*. "Enjoy your day in the meadow, Ovejita," said the sheepherder as he twined **sprigs** of bluebonnets around her neck.

The sheepherder kept a watchful eye on his sheep, especially the lambs. He was determined to protect them from the coyote

---

1   (Oh veh HEE tah) An *ovejita* is a "small sheep."
2   (mehs KEE teh) A *mesquite* is a spiny tree with feathery foliage.
3   (sah KAH teh) *Zacate* is grass or hay.

that lived nearby. Ovejita often heard him complain to himself about "that up-to-no-good Señor[4] Coyote."

Later, Ovejita wandered over to the low stone wall on one end of the meadow. She wanted to eat the delicious berries that grew over the stones. She was far away from the devoted sheepherder now. Little did she know that the **cunning** Señor Coyote was hiding behind the wall.

When Ovejita came closer, Señor Coyote leaped over the wall.

"Aha! Ovejita, there you are!"

Ovejita shivered under her fleece. She was nose to nose with the dreaded Señor Coyote. Ovejita was scared. But she smiled and said, "Baaa! *Buenos días,*[5] Señor Coyote. You're looking sleek and handsome today."

Señor Coyote grinned, showing a mouthful of pointy teeth. "And you look nice and fat. I'm going to eat you up!"

Ovejita's heart beat fast, and she wanted to turn and run. But she knew Señor Coyote would catch her. So she had to think fast.

"*¡Híjola!*[6]" replied Ovejita with a laugh, "You don't understand, dear Señor Coyote. I'm not as fat as I appear. I'm really skinny under all this **fleece.** The sheepherder hasn't **sheared** me yet. That's why I look so fat. Let me graze in this lovely meadow, and soon you'll enjoy a feast fit for a king."

Señor Coyote looked at her fleece. "*Bueno.*[7] I'll wait a little longer. But hurry and get fat."

Ovejita was free, but she knew Señor Coyote would be back. So while she grazed, she thought out a plan.

Time passed, and soon Señor Coyote returned. "Aha! Ovejita, there you are! You're fat now, and I'm going to gobble you up!"

"Baaa!" bleated Ovejita. "I look plump and round. But there's something that's even more plump and so round that it could roll right through the meadow. It's cheese, and it's so

---

4   (SEHN yor) *Señor* means "mister."
5   (V'WEH nohs DEE ahs) *Buenos días* means "good day" or "good morning."
6   (EE hoh lah) *Híjola* means "goodness sakes."
7   (V'WEH noh) *Bueno* means "good."

delicious. I was going to get some for myself, but I'll share it with you if you like."

Señor Coyote's pointy teeth shone as he spoke to Ovejita. "Where can we get some of this tasty cheese?"

"There's a full moon this evening. That's the best time of the month to find cheese. Meet me at the **lagoon** tonight."

"*Bueno*. I'll see you then," he growled.

That night, Ovejita waited near the edge of the lagoon. Soon Señor Coyote came along. He sat next to Ovejita and began complaining.

"I waited all day for this cheese. I'm so hungry. Where is this cheese? It had better be good, or I'll gobble you up."

Ovejita caught her breath in at those last words. But she tried to stay calm as she gazed into the water. The moon reflected on the still water. "*Mira,*[8] Señor Coyote. The big, round cheese is hiding in the lagoon. Baaa—but we've got it now. The cheese can't escape with both of us here."

Señor Coyote's eyes glittered as he stared at the moon's reflection. "That's a really big cheese."

"Oh yes, Señor Coyote. There's plenty for us both. Baaa—but we'll have to catch the cheese before it drifts away."

"*Bueno*. How do we catch this cheese?"

Ovejita looked at the rope by her side. The *vaquero*[9] loaned me his lasso. I'll throw the rope into the water, and you, Señor Coyote, will jump in, and together we'll pull out the cheese. Then we'll divide it in half and have a late dinner."

Señor Coyote grinned, and his teeth **glinted** like two rows of knives. "*Bueno*. This is a good plan, Ovejita." He licked his chops hungrily and took a step toward her.

Ovejita knew he was hungry, and she tried to distract him. "*Mira*—the cheese is drifting away."

Señor Coyote turned and stared at the moon's reflection as it slipped farther into the lagoon. Then he turned back to her.

Ovejita gave a little leap and bleated, "Baaa! Hurry! Jump! Maaa—*Mamacita!* Jump! Jump into the lagoon and catch the cheese before it escapes."

---

8   (MEE rah) *Mira* means "look."

9   (vah KEH roh) A *vaquero* is a cowboy or cowhand.

With a run and a mighty leap, Señor Coyote soared over the **shimmering** water.

SPLASH!

He came up for air and swam towards the reflection. Though he paddled fast, the **elusive** "cheese" rolled just out of his reach.

Ovejita watched as Señor Coyote gave a mighty growl and shot ahead with his mouth open to catch the cheese. But all he got for his effort was a mouthful of water. The moon's reflection scattered in the **churning** waves. Ovejita turned and ran fast. She ran all the way back to the safe, cozy barn.

Señor Coyote coughed and sputtered. Then he stared at the reflection. "What sort of cheese is this? What's happening?" He looked up and saw the round, yellow moon. It shone down on the lagoon.

"No fair, no fair! I've been tricked!" Señor Coyote yipped in frustration. "Ohhh—this water is so cold that my teeth are trembling."

He swam to the edge of the lagoon and pulled himself out of the water. "Wait till I get my paws on that Ovejita. She'll pay for her lies."

Drops of water turned silver in the moonlight as Señor Coyote shook his fur. Then he sat, pointed his nose to the moon, and howled every note in his **repertoire.**

"Oooo-Ooo-ooo! WoooWoo-woooo! Yip-Yowwwoo!"

His sad solo echoed through the countryside. But Ovejita heard nothing. She was far away, snug in the barn.

Holding Up the World

Early one morning, Ovejita followed the trail that led to a cliff. She knew a place where wildflowers and *zacate* grew in **profusion.** As she grazed on the ledge that jutted out halfway up the cliff, Ovejita saw Señor Coyote coming up the trail. He trotted along, his nose pointed at the ground, searching, as always, for something to eat.

Ovejita bleated and ran in circles. A steep, rocky cliff loomed above the ledge. The trail was the only way down.

"Señor Coyote will find me, and this time he'll show no mercy. What shall I do?"

Ovejita thought and thought as she stood on the ledge. She kicked at some pebbles and peeked over the edge of the ledge. She smiled. "I have the perfect plan."

Señor Coyote found Ovejita beneath the ledge where the rocky cliff formed a small cave. Ovejita lay on her back, her hooves **braced** against the overhanging ledge.

"I see you, Ovejita. You can't escape," growled Señor Coyote. "Come out of there or I'll come in after you. *¡Ándale, córrele!*"[10]

"I can't come out. The sheepherder asked me to hold up the world. He went for help and promised to reward me for my efforts. But I'm s-o-o-o tired. I can't hold up the world much longer."

Señor Coyote moved closer. "Now's my chance. I'll enjoy a nice meal after all."

"*¡Híjola, híjola!* How can you think of food at a time like this? If the world falls, there won't be another meal. Not today, not tomorrow, or ever. If the world falls, it will be the end of everything."

Señor Coyote laughed. "That's ridiculous. Let down your hooves and you'll see. The world won't fall." Ovejita moved her hooves a little, and a trail of pebbles showered her. "Ohhh! Maaa-*Mamacita*—I'm losing my grip."

Señor Coyote looked at the pebbles. "Indeed, the world really is falling!" he cried in alarm.

"We're doomed," cried Ovejita. "I can't last much longer. You're so strong, Señor Coyote. If you'll hold the world on your strong paws, I'll go tell the sheepherder to bring you a nice fat hen for your reward."

"*Bueno,*" said Señor Coyote. Move aside, Ovejita. "Let me hold the world."

Ovejita let down her hooves and **scampered** out of the cave. "You're so brave and strong."

---

10   (AHN dah leh, KOHR reh leh) *¡Ándale, córrele!* means "run for it."

Señor Coyote put his paws against the ledge and pushed with all his strength. "Yes, I know. Now go get my hen. And hurry because I'm really hungry."

Ovejita peeked over the ledge. "Do you have a good grip?"

"*Sí, sí*—go find the sheepherder."

Ovejita leaped down the trail and ran fast all the way back to the barnyard.

Señor Coyote waited beneath the ledge the rest of the morning. He grew tired and thirsty. His paws were stiff and numb. His back was aching, and his throat felt dusty and dry. "*¡Rayos!* [11] If the world is going to fall, then let it fall. I can't stand this pain any longer."

He let down his tender paws and crawled out of the cave. He lay on the ledge and waited for the big fall. But the fall didn't happen, and the world didn't come to an end.

Señor Coyote yelped in frustration. "*¡Rayos y truenos!*[12] Tricked again. When I catch that Ovejita, I won't listen to her lies. No! She'll pay for tricking me."

When the moon came up, Señor Coyote howled. His song was sad and lonesome and rang through the hills and meadows. Finally it reached the barnyard where Ovejita slept on a soft bed of hay.

Chickens in a Tree

Late one night, Ovejita heard fluttering and clucking sounds in the barn. She opened her eyes and looked around.

Gallina,[13] a hen with shining red-brown feathers, fluttered around the barn. She was nervous and upset about something.

Ovejita hurried to her friend. "What's wrong, Gallina?"

"Coyote was here tonight. If it wasn't for the good-hearted sheepherder, I'd be nothing but a pile of crumpled feathers. Señor Coyote's after me, Ovejita. He stared at me with those awful, glittering eyes. I clucked and fluttered until the sheepherder

---

11   (RAH yohs) *¡Rayos!* literally means "Lightning flashes!" It is an exclamatory phrase meaning "Darn it!"

12   (TRUEH nohs) *Truenos* literally means "thunderclaps." It is an exclamatory phrase meaning "darn it" or "good heavens."

13   (gah YEE nah) A *gallina* is a hen.

came running. But that Señor Coyote—he'll be back. I can feel it in my bones."

"Easy, Gallina," said Ovejita with a calming baa. "Don't lose any of your beautiful feathers over this. I'll think of something."

Gallina flew onto Ovejita's back. "Can we really stop him? Why is he so cruel?"

Ovejita shook her head. "Baaa-ba-bad. He's just naturally bad. Don't worry, Gallina. Something will be done about Señor Coyote. The sheepherder set a trap in the meadow."

Gallina fluttered her wings. "I saw the sheepherder tie some stones in the mesquite tree. But Señor Coyote won't fall for it."

"But when the sun's straight up, we might be able to trick Señor Coyote. I have a plan that will get old Señor Coyote. But I need your help, Gallina."

When the hot summer sun was straight up in the Texas sky, Señor Coyote knew a stray sheep might seek shelter under the mesquite tree. He found Ovejita resting under the tree.

"Aha! I've got you at long last! And now I'll have a fine feast."

Ovejita hoped Señor Coyote couldn't hear her heart pounding beneath her fleecy coat. "Why would you want one small sheep when you could dine on a dozen fine, fat hens?"

Señor Coyote shook his head in agreement.

"Look—look up there, in the tree. Do you see the hens? I tied up 12 and saved them especially for you, Señor Coyotito."[14]

He looked up. "The sun is in my eyes."

Gallina fluttered on the limb. "Cluck-cluck."

Señor Coyote danced in a circle. "Happy, happy day! Oh, what a fine feast is waiting for me." He looked at Ovejita. "How do we get those chickens down from the tree?"

Ovejita stood next to a long rope that hung down from the tree. "I'll pull the rope, and down will come your tasty treat. But first, come a little closer, Señor Coyotito."

"*Bueno.* I'm here—I'm here."

"Are you ready, Señor Coyotito?"

"*¡Sí, sí!* Hurry."

---

14   (Coh yoh TEE toh) *Coyotito* means "little coyote."

Ovejita smiled. "Would you like one chicken at a time or all of the hens at once?"

Señor Coyote hopped in a circle. "All at once—all at once. And be quick about it."

Ovejita took the rope in her mouth and pulled—hard. Then she stepped back.

Gallina clucked and fluttered down onto Ovejita's fleecy back. And 11 stones fell on Señor Coyote—all at once.

Ovejita, with Gallina hanging on tight, ran fast all the way back to the barnyard.

Painfully crawling from under the stones, Señor Coyote limped away from the pile. He yelped as he headed for his cave in the hills to rest and recover from his bruises.

That night, his **forlorn** howls were heard in the hills and meadows and barnyard where Ovejita lay on a new bed of soft, sweet-smelling hay. She dreamed of grazing on berries, *zacate,* and wildflowers in her beautiful Texas countryside.

INSIGHTS

Señor Coyote appears in many Mexican and Southwestern folktales. Coyote's name is taken from the Aztec (Nahautl) word *coyotl.* Folktales from Mexico and the Southwestern United States often portray him as a villain. Coyote is everyone's enemy, and, as a result, people like to see coyote outwitted.

Cunning and mischievous, Señor Coyote is a type of trickster. Tricksters are found in tales all over the world. These tales usually have unexpected twists and surprise endings. Often the strong, stingy, or stupid are taken in by the trickster's antics. However, the trickster can fall into the trap of another, more clever character.

Señor Coyote's rival is often a sheep but is sometimes a fox, rabbit, raccoon, or roadrunner. For example, in another version of this tale, it is a fox who convinces Coyote to watch a huge "cheese."

There is a long tradition of sheepherding in Mexico and the Southwestern United States. The sheepherders in these regions are devoted in the solitary job of herding sheep and protecting them from predators like the coyote. Some sheepherders and ranchers keep dogs to help scare off coyotes while a few farmers keep a llama for their sheep's protection.

Spain was first to produce a special breed of wool-bearing domestic sheep. The fleece on the modern domestic sheep is soft and varies in color: white, beige, light brown, and black. It is sheared in late spring or summer by experts who travel from ranch to ranch.

Sheep are gentle, sweet-natured animals. In Mexico and the Southwestern United States, they are popular with children and adults and are featured in holiday pageants. Sheep are herbivores and like to graze on grass, hay, wildflowers, clover, berries, and weeds. They can even eat weeds that are poisonous to other animals.

A popular saying in Mexico is "Don't think that the moon is made of cheese because it looks round." The saying comes from the first of these three folktales. It is used as a warning not to be fooled by appearances much like the phrase, "All that glitters is not gold."

The word *mesquite* comes from the Aztec word *mizquitl*. The mesquite tree with its delicate evergreen foliage thrives in the deserts of Mexico and the Southwest. This tree has spreading, dark limbs. The lowest limbs are often quite close to the ground.

Ovejita's favorite flower is the bluebonnet, the state flower of Texas. It is a beautiful flower with deep blue-violet petals. A single bluebonnet flower looks like a small bouquet because it has many tiny flowers on one stem. The bluebonnet would look striking against all colors of fleece on the domestic sheep.

The Badger and the Rattlesnake

VOCABULARY PREVIEW

The following words appear in the story. Review the list and get to know the words before you read the story.

contemplated—thought about; considered
countered—responded; retorted
gaze—look at; stare
implored—begged; insisted
lumbering—moving along heavily; trudging
lure—tempt
naive—childlike; trusting
perish—die
perplexing—puzzling; strange
plea—request; prayer
precisely—exactly
predicament—difficult situation; trial
rivulets—small streams
sweltering—hot; stifling
twitching—quivering; moving jerkily

MAIN CHARACTERS

Señor Snake—a rattlesnake
Badger—a good-natured badger
Señor Coyote—a coyote

The Badger and the Rattlesnake

A tale set in Arizona

One good turn deserves another,
or so believes Badger. But can Badger
convince the mischievous Señor Coyote?

One long, hot afternoon, a rattlesnake searched for shade from the Arizona sun. The snake spotted a stone and tried to squeeze himself underneath it. As he wedged himself deeper, the stone tumbled onto his tail. The rattler tugged and pulled, but he couldn't free himself.

A young badger came walking along, sniffing the warm air. The snake called out to him, "*Amigo,*[1] come and push this heavy rock off my tail, and I'll be eternally grateful."

The good-natured badger, not wishing to see a fellow desert dweller **perish** in the **sweltering** heat, hurried over to the snake. "Take heart, my friend. I'll free you in *un momentito.*"[2] He gave the rock a mighty shove, and out came the snake.

Freed from the stone, the rattlesnake immediately positioned himself nose to nose with the badger and prepared to strike. "Now I have you where I want you. The long wait under the stone has made me hungry. So now, my foolish friend, I will bite you on your tender nose."

The badger dug his strong claws into the sand and froze. If he ran or moved or even twitched a muscle, the snake would surely strike. So he decided it would be best to use his wits.

---

1   (ah MEE goh) An *amigo* is a friend.
2   (oon moh mehn TEE toh) *Un momentito* means "one small moment."

"With due respect, Señor[3] Snake, this is not the right plan of action."

The snake stared at him with his small, mean eyes. "What do you mean by that?"

"I acted in good faith," replied the badger. "Is this the way you repay my kindness?"

"I was a prisoner for too long," **countered** the snake. "And now it is your fault that I must strike."

"My fault? How is that possible?"

The snake raised his head and looked down at the badger. "I waited all afternoon for you to arrive. If you had come sooner, I wouldn't be so hungry. Then you'd be free to shuffle around the desert doing whatever it is that badgers do."

The young badger was taken aback and replied, "That may be true, Señor Snake. But I say it is wrong to repay good with bad. After all, one good turn deserves another good turn. Isn't that right and true?"

The cruel snake laughed. "That may be true for some creatures—for some **naive** creatures. But where I come from, it is quite the opposite. I say that good is always repaid with bad."

The young badger knew the end was near, and so he made one last desperate **plea**. "I don't know that saying, Señor Snake. Perhaps we should seek another opinion in this matter."

"All wise creatures would agree with me," the snake told him. "However, I'll gladly add to your suffering and seek a judge."

The badger looked all around and saw a horse trudging along, kicking up sand. "Oh, Señor Caballo,[4] listen to me. We are seeking a judge and you will serve us well."

Señor Caballo listened, his ears **twitching** and his tail swishing. "It's true, *amigos*," he replied. "Good is always repaid with bad. I can illustrate this point. In my youth, I used to work for the *vaqueros*.[5] I helped them rope calves and could outrun any steer. The *vaqueros* used up all my strength and never showed any appreciation, but I never complained."

---

3   (Seh NYOHR) *Señor* means "mister."

4   (kah BAH yoh) A *caballo* is a horse.

5   (vah KEH rohs) *Vaqueros* are cowboys or cowhands.

The horse whinnied and then sighed. "And so my life passed me by. And my reward? Now that I'm old, my legs are no longer able to bear the weight of a *vaquero*. And so I've been abandoned and left here in the desert. Yes, good is always repaid with bad."

The young badger grew cold though the sun burned overhead. "Señor Caballo is sincere," he said nervously. "But let's ask for another opinion."

Before long an ox, huge but bone-thin, came **lumbering** along.

"Oh, good Señor Ox," cried the badger "I need your assistance in an important matter."

Señor Ox listened as he chewed his cud and **contemplated** the badger's **predicament.** "Ah, yes. Good is indeed repaid with bad. Once I was like you, my youthful badger—ready to help my fellow beings. I was innocent of the ways of this world. I was strong, able-bodied, and obedient. I plowed all day and the sweat rolled off my back in **rivulets.** But I never caused the farmer a moment of grief. And now that I'm too old for the plow, I've been left here in the desert. And the vultures circle my head, waiting for me to die. One day soon, I'll be a pile of white bones on the red-brown sand."

"So, I'm right," hissed the snake. "All creatures agree with me."

"Only two have agreed," the anxious badger pointed out. "I believe we should seek one more opinion."

The snake turned its head toward the setting sun. A coyote came swiftly along, ready to enjoy the oncoming twilight. "Here comes a fine desert sage. Let him be the final judge."

The badger **implored** the coyote to listen intently, which he did—wagging his tail back and forth.

"So," hissed the snake, "what is your judgment?"

The coyote stared with piercing yellow eyes. "This is indeed a complex and **perplexing** problem. I must look into this carefully to weigh the issue."

The snake met his gaze. "What do you mean by that?"

Señor Coyote turned to the badger. "Show me **precisely** where you found Señor Snake. It is possible, my young friend, that he was not truly trapped. It is possible that he wished to **lure** you into a trap."

The snake shook his tail hard. The young badger trembled at the sound of rattling.

"What? That is untrue!" shouted the snake. "Of course I was trapped. Let me demonstrate."

The snake wiggled under the rock and allowed the coyote to roll the stone over him.

Señor Coyote looked at the snake. "Is this the way you were imprisoned?"

"Yes, of course," hissed the snake. "And it is impossible to escape."

Señor Coyote turned to the young badger. "And is this the way Señor Snake was trapped when you rescued him?"

"Oh, yes," said the badger.

The coyote smiled. "Well, now, my young badger, I have returned the favor I owed you."

The puzzled snake called out, "And what do you mean by that?"

Señor Coyote squinted into the red and gold Arizona sunset and remembered. "It was on a long, hot day such as this. There was no water to be found for miles around. Not a drop. I became quite dizzy and lay panting out near Red Mesa. The hot wind blew a desert song around me and I thought I would surely die."

The wind stirred as Señor Coyote paused to scratch his chin. "Then along you came, my young badger friend. You dug a hole with your strong claws. You dug long and deep. Suddenly, the hole filled with water. Muddy water, true. But it satisfied my thirst and I was rescued."

The young badger smiled. "So you agree, *amigo*. One good turn deserves another good turn."

"In this case, yes." Senor Coyote stood and stretched. "And now, *amigo*, shall we leave this place?"

And the two friends began walking off together.

"But you must release me," called the rattlesnake. "Don't you know the old saying, 'Good is repaid with bad'?"

Señor Coyote turned to **gaze** at the snake. "No, I don't know that saying. But I do know the saying 'One good deed deserves another good deed,' and that's why I'm helping Badger."

"But who will help me?" protested the snake.

Señor Coyote thought for a moment. "Well, that depends on how many friends you have. One of them might come along and recall a past kindness you once showed."

"Yes," agreed Badger, "for one good deed deserves another good deed."

And the two friends walked off together.

INSIGHTS

Animal tales abound in Mexico. Some of the most well-known tales are about Señor Coyote. This infamous doglike creature usually appears as a troublemaker. Food is everything to him, and he goes to no end in its pursuit. However, in "The Badger and the Rattlesnake," he is the hero. He shrewdly deals with the rattlesnake and helps the badger get justice.

At the center of most animal tales is an ongoing rivalry. Coyote and Sis Fox are well-known rivals. In one tale, Coyote is bent on revenge when he finds the fox. The fox is playing with a hornet's nest and claims that the nest is a class of boys that she is being paid to keep an eye on. She calls it a "blab school." Food is mentioned, and the coyote volunteers to watch the "boys" while she goes searching for a couple of chickens. When the "boys" stop their humming, coyote shakes them up and has to run for the pond to escape their stings.

The badger and the coyote in this tale work together to outwit the rattlesnake. However, in real life they are not friends or hunting partners. Badgers like to dig rabbits and other prey out of their burrows. Badgers have poor eyesight and sometimes don't notice that the coyote sneaks up to the rabbit's escape hole. Often, when the rabbit tries to escape, the thieving coyote snatches the prize and runs off with it.

Early in this story, when the rattlesnake is first rescued from under the rock, he tells the badger that he is going to bite him on the nose. The badger's nose is his weak spot. The badger's fur is so thick that a rattlesnake's fangs can't sink into it deep enough to cause damage. But even a light swat on the nose would kill him.

RIGHT AND WRONG

From Such a Stick Comes Such a Splinter

Good Compadre, Bad Compadre

"How should we treat other people?" "What are the consequences of mistreatment?" These are the questions answered in stories about right and wrong.

The danger of greed is a common theme in Mexican American folklore. Many stories contain characters who love money and property so much that they deceive others. As in folktales around the world, such characters usually learn the hard way—and we readers get a laugh at their expense.

As you read the following tales, decide which actions the storyteller believes are wrong and which are right.

From Such a Stick Comes Such a Splinter

VOCABULARY PREVIEW

The following words appear in the story. Review the list and get to know the words before you read the story.

exception—unusual case; oddity
generations—age groups
heirlooms—inherited objects
inheritance—things handed down; legacy
ladled—spooned; served
pathetic—sad; pitiful
tattered—shredded; ragged
whittling—carving; paring

MAIN CHARACTERS

Juanito—a young boy
Papá—Juanito's grandfather
Mother—Juanito's mother
Father—Juanito's father

From Such a Stick Comes Such a Splinter

"What's in the box you're throwing away, Mother? And why does Grandpa sleep in the cold barn?" A young boy's questions lead to a surprising discovery.

Once long ago in the land called Colorado, there lived a family. This family included a man, his wife, a young boy named Juanito[1], and an old man who was almost blind and deaf. In those days it was not uncommon for several **generations** to live together in one house. Usually, they lived happily and worked together. The younger folk cared for the older folk and were grateful for their wisdom.

Juanito's family was an **exception.** The old and young didn't work together. The old man was treated very poorly by his son and daughter-in-law. At mealtime, the daughter-in-law never gave the old man enough soup and often forced him to sit on a small stool in the corner of the room.

"Your hands shake so much, you will spill the soup on my tablecloth," she would say. And usually she was right. He could hardly hold the spoon, so he lifted the bowl to his lips. Sometimes the bowl would reach his mouth, but often it slipped out of his hands and dropped on the floor.

The old man's son mistreated the old man as well. "You are always in the way, Papá," his son would say. "Why can't you just go to your corner and leave us alone?"

---

1   (Wah NEE toh) The name *Juanito* is "Johnny" in Spanish.

One day Juanito's mother came down from the attic dragging a large wooden box. The boy studied the box over. "What is that?" he asked.

"Just an old trunk. I'm getting rid of this ancient dust catcher once and for all," she said.

Juanito followed his mother into the living room. "Where did you get that box?"

His mother set the **tattered** trunk next to the fireplace. "Oh, for goodness sakes, Juanito. Why must you ask so many questions? It's just an old useless box that Grandma and Grandpa gave us years ago."

Juanito stared at the box but said nothing.

His mother dusted off her hands. "The box will make good firewood. At least it will be good for something. That's more than I can say for that good-for-nothing grandfather of yours."

Juanito followed his mother into the kitchen. "Why did Grandma and Grandpa give the trunk to you?"

His mother sighed. "Juanito, it's just an old box—a family chest. You save things in it. Then you give the things to people in your family."

"That's right, Juanito," his father agreed. "It's just a shabby old thing—not worth much anymore. We sold the good things, the **heirlooms,** a long time ago. The things in that old chest were our **inheritance.** Now run along and play," he said without looking up from the branch he was **whittling.**

"Heir-looms. In-her-i-tance," Juanito repeated. He liked saying new words, especially long words. He learned many new words while listening to his grandfather's stories. Often, late in the evening, Juanito's grandfather told him stories about his early days in Colorado.

"May I have the box?" Juanito asked. "I need it for something important."

"That old trunk won't make a good toy box," his mother told him.

His father dropped the branch that he was whittling. "Ouch, I got a splinter," he said, looking at his thumb. "Go ahead. Go

ahead and take the box, but don't expect us to spend all of our
pesos[2] filling it up with toys."

Juanito dragged the trunk into the kitchen.

"Don't make a mess on the floor," his mother warned.
"I already have too much work to do around here." She frowned
at the elderly man sitting at a small table in the corner of the
kitchen.

Juanito pulled the box toward his Grandpa. "Look Grandpa.
This is mine now."

Juanito's Grandpa held a big wooden spoon in his fist on
top of the old wooden table. He was ready and waiting for his
meal. He looked sad as he stared at the wooden chest out of the
corner of his eye.

"Old man, you know I hate when you do that," Juanito's
mother said as she grabbed the spoon from Grandpa's hand and
slammed it hard on the table. The spoon splintered into three
pieces.

"Now look what you did," she added. She walked to the
cupboard. "That's the second thing you've broken this week!"

Juanito looked at his grandfather's sad, almost **pathetic**
face. Tears ran down the old man's cheeks. The boy then picked
up the pieces of the spoon and began tying them together with
scraps of string. He carefully placed the spoon in the chest when
he finished mending it.

Juanito's mother placed an old chipped spoon on the small
table. "Here, old man. You can use this one. And this old cracked
bowl will do just fine. You'll probably break it too."

Juanito's mother **ladled** some cold beans into Grandpa's
bowl. Then she tossed down an old tortilla and half a glass
of water.

The old man looked up at her with his large dark eyes.
Juanito sat across from him and watched him eat. "Tell me
about the time you sailed down the Colorado River, Grandpa. I
love that story."

Grandpa smiled. "Oh, that was a wonderful adventure,
mijo.[3] We were taking some chickens to an old mining town.

2   (PEH sohs) The *peso* is a Mexican monetary unit. It is similar to the dollar.
3   (MEE hoh) *Mijo* means "my son."

We were planning to sell them, you know. And we had this raft . . ."

Juanito's father looked up from his soup. "Not that old story again. Papá, you're getting as old as the Colorado River, always talking about those long-gone days."

"He's as old as Pike's Peak!" Juanito's mother laughed.

Juanito's father frowned at Grandpa. "Don't fill Juanito's head with your foolish stories."

But Grandpa continued. "Juanito, the raft carried us for several miles down the river. The chickens were so scared that they hid under a tarp I brought with me . . ."

"Juanito, it's bedtime," interrupted Juanito's father as he stoked the fire. "It's time to take Papá out to the barn."

Juanito stood up and reached for his grandpa's large, rough hand and led the old man reluctantly to the barn. The wind blew hard, and Juanito felt a few raindrops. Juanito heard his grandpa sniff when they reached the barn. He looked up and saw tears running down the old man's cheek.

"Why do they make you sleep in the barn, Grandpa?"

His grandfather shivered. "Because I'm old and of no use to them."

Juanito said goodnight to the old man and closed the barn door. Then he ran back to the house. "Oh, it's so cold out there," he told his mother when he walked into the kitchen. He rubbed the chill out of his hands. "Grandpa could use another blanket."

His mother took down a blanket from the linen closet in the hall. "Take him this old wool blanket. It's a bit moth-eaten, but it'll do."

"Papá, would you cut the blanket in half?" the boy asked.

His father looked puzzled. "Just take Papá the blanket."

"No, Papá. I want to save half of it and put it in the trunk."

"Why would you do that, son?"

"I'm saving old things. I already have the broken spoon and an old chipped bowl."

"Whatever for?" asked Juanito's mother with a scowl.

"I'm saving them for you. Someday you'll be old like Grandpa. You'll need these old things."

Juanito's father looked at his wife. Then he turned to his son and said, "Bring Papá back to the house."

When Grandpa returned from the barn, Juanito's mother placed a hot cup of tea on the big table. Juanito's father set a new spoon next to a teacup.

"Sit with us, Papá," Juanito's father said. "We were just having a snack before going to sleep."

Juanito's mother smiled at Grandpa. "I put some clean sheets and blankets on the couch for you. It's nice and warm in there by the fireplace."

As time passed, Juanito listened to his grandfather's stories as often as he liked. And nobody scolded or complained when the old man spilled a little tea or food.

INSIGHTS

Versions of "From Such a Stick Comes Such a Splinter" are popular all over the world. The tale is told in central Europe, in Africa and Asia, and among the Native American people. It is one of many fable-like stories told in Mexico and the Southwestern United States.

The Mohawks, a Native American tribe, tell a version of this story that differs slighty. In that version, a man tells his son to take his grandfather into the forest and to leave him there. The man hands a blanket to his son and asks him to wrap it around the old man's shoulders. The boy tears the blanket in half and wraps half of it around his grandfather. He returns to his father with the other half, and when his father sees him, he asks his son what he plans to do with it. The boy responds by saying, "I'll wrap this half of the blanket around your shoulders when I leave you in the forest." When the father hears these words, he feels remorseful for how he's treated the old man.

The title "From Such a Stick Comes Such a Splinter" is a popular saying in Mexico. It is like saying "He is cut from the same cloth" or "The apple doesn't fall far from the tree."

Like other fables, this tale contains a moral. It illustrates how the young should treat the old. It also suggests that parents should be careful about how they act in front of their children. The stick in the title represents a parent while the splinter represents a child.

Good Compadre, Bad Compadre

VOCABULARY PREVIEW

The following words appear in the story. Review the list and get to know the words before you read the story.

abandon—leave behind; desert
abundance—endless supply; plenty
amethyst—a clear purple gemstone
craggy—rocky; rugged
deceptive—misleading; false
dismounted—got off
doffed—removed; took off
dwelling—home; shelter
exaggerates—overstates; embellishes
gourds—hard, outer rind of plants used to store water
groped—blindly searched
insinuation—hint; suggestive comment
nuzzled—rubbed; pushed gently
prosperity—wealth; riches
rebuff—rejection; put-down
whinnied—neighed; cried

MAIN CHARACTERS

Horacio—rich rancher
Ernesto—poor farmer
Tessa—Ernesto's wife

Good Compadre, Bad Compadre

Poor Ernesto and his wife Tessa lead simple
and contented lives until Horacio plants the
seeds of greed in Ernesto's mind.
Can the two resist the temptations of wealth?

In a small town in New Mexico there lived two *compadres*[1]
—one rich and one poor. The rich *compadre,* Horacio, was
a greedy rancher who lived on a large ranch surrounded by
20 acres of land. He owned one hundred cows, two dozen
chickens, eighty sheep, and over one hundred mustangs.

The poor *compadre,* Ernesto, was an honest, hard-working
farmer who lived in a small, ancient adobe **dwelling** surrounded
by flowers. Larkspur, purple clover, corn, and tomatoes grew in
abundance on his single acre of land. He owned one cow, one
chicken, one sheep, and a burro.

Early one morning, Ernesto sat in the barnyard milking his
cow. He looked up to see Horacio riding a fine horse down the
narrow path that led to the farm. To Ernesto's surprise, Horacio
carelessly allowed his mustang to crush the ripe tomatoes and
trample the corn.

"*Buenos días,*"[2] Horacio said as he slid off the horse and
greeted his *compadre* with a smile and an embrace. "It's good to
see you looking so well."

Ernesto frowned. "Well, I haven't changed much since
yesterday."

Horacio ignored the remark and turned to the cow. "I see
you still have your cow, though she's getting quite old."

"*Sí, compadre.* I still have the same cow I had yesterday.
She may be a day older, but she still gives plenty of milk, as

---

1   (kohm PAH drehs) The word *compadre* means "godfather" or "friend."
2   (V'WEH nohs DEE ahs) *Buenos días* means "good day" or "good morning."

anyone with eyes can see. My Manzanita[3] is a magnificent cow. She's a gift from heaven."

Horacio looked at the cow's shining coat. He stared at the bucket of creamy milk. "Let me help you out, friend. I'll give you fifty *pesos*[4] for your cow. She'll live to a contented old age in my pastures."

Ernesto patted the cow's silky side. "Oh, no, *compadre*. Manzanita is my only cow, and without her, how would my family survive?"

Horacio blew through his teeth. Then he said, "Tell you what. I'll give you five of my cows because we're friends. That's a good opportunity for you to improve your circumstances. What do you say to that?"

Ernesto moved closer to Horacio and looked straight into his eyes. "I may be poor with none of the advantages of **prosperity**, but I know a thing or two. And I know Manzanita is never dry. She gives more milk than five of your cows. She's been good to my family, and I won't **abandon** her just because she's growing old. So tell me, what do you say to that?"

Without another word, Horacio climbed onto his horse, a golden brown mustang. He pulled the reins hard, and the animal **whinnied** in pain.

Ernesto now recognized the mustang. He saw the fear in the animal's dark eyes, the sweat on the fine coat. "*Compadre,* let this horse rest," Ernesto demanded. "He needs a rubdown and blanket so he won't catch a chill."

Horacio ignored these comments, spurred the horse, and rode off so fast that dust swirled around Ernesto.

"If anything happens to that horse," Ernesto shouted, "you'll have to deal with me!"

Ernesto coughed and pulled Manzanita away from the dust. "¡*Santitos!*[5] That greedy man wants what belongs to me. I don't know why, Manzanita. He owns 305 animals, but he doesn't care for even one of them. He cheated me out of

---

3   (Mahn sah NEE tah) Manzanita, the name of Ernesto's cow, is the name of a shrub that grows in New Mexico.

4   (PEH sohs) The *peso* is a monetary unit in Mexico. It is similar to the dollar.

5   (sahn TEE tohs) *Santitos* is an exclamatory phrase meaning "dear saints."

my beautiful mustang Encanto. Did you see how he mistreats my horse?"

Manzanita mooed in her sad, low voice. She gazed at Ernesto with mournful eyes.

Ernesto rubbed her nose. "Don't worry, Manzanita. I'll never sell you. It's unthinkable."

Later that morning Ernesto and his wife, Tessa, carried milk, butter, and cheese to the open market. Horacio was already there. He greeted Ernesto with another big smile and embrace. Ernesto pulled away, but Horacio ignored the **rebuff.**

"So good to see you, friend." Horacio turned to Tessa. He **doffed** his hat and held it over his heart. "*Buenos días,* friend."

Tessa nodded without smiling or speaking.

"I'm happy to see you looking so well. You look lovely in that *rebozo*[6] and pretty dress." He bowed to her.

Tessa looked disgusted. "You've seen this *rebozo* 20 times and the dress one hundred times. It was woven from overpriced wool you sold to us two years ago."

Horacio quickly turned to Ernesto. "I see you brought milk, butter, and cheese. Do you think you'll have any luck?"

"Yes, friend. People come from far and near to buy our milk and butter. And they can't resist our cheese—so rich and *sabroso.*[7] Just one taste and they're in heaven."

Ernesto cut a slice from the round of cheese. "Take some, *compadre.*"

Horacio took the whole round of cheese and left the single slice. "It's such a shame, Ernesto. You and your Tessa work so hard and yet barely survive."

Ernesto frowned. "We get by. Of course, we would do better if some people weren't so greedy."

Horacio ignored the **insinuation.** "There's a village in the mountains where people pay ten *pesos* for a single pair of sandals. Your cow is so fat that you could make a hundred pairs of sandals from her hide."

Ernesto counted in his head. "Ten times one hundred— that's one thousand *pesos.*"

---

6   (reh VOH soh) A *rebozo* is a shawl.

7   (sah V'ROH soh) *Sabroso* means "delicious."

"Yes friend. You'd be rich." Horacio stuffed his mouth with the cheese. Bits of cheese clung to his mustache. "Ummm. Good cheese." And he left.

Ernesto stared after him. "Did you hear that, Tessa? Ten *pesos* for a pair of sandals."

Tessa took a block of cheese out of her basket and placed it on the empty plate. "That *puerco*![8] He ate the whole cheese. Don't listen to anything he says. He always lies."

Ernesto shrugged. "He **exaggerates** a little."

"He tells lies," Tessa insisted. "I don't believe anything he says. Let's not waste time talking about him. Look—here comes a customer."

That night, sleep wouldn't come to Ernesto. He lay in bed and listened to a coyote's lonesome song. One thousand pesos would buy so many things for Tessa, their little daughter, and the farm. He worked hard, and Tessa worked hard. Why shouldn't they have a few new things?

Early the next morning, Ernesto walked into the barn. Manzanita turned to look at him. Her sad eyes seemed to say "I know what you must do, Ernesto, and I understand."

Ernesto thought of the days long ago when Manzanita was born. He recalled his father's words. "She's a beautiful calf, *mijo*.[9] She's yours to keep. Always remember, if you take care of your animals, they will repay you a thousandfold."

A thousandfold. The words echoed in his mind. "¡Santitos! Forgive me, Manzanita." He patted her side. "After all you've given to my family. It's impossible. It's unthinkable. I can't do it. I won't do it. There must be another way."

Ernesto thought for a few moments. "Yes—there is another way."

He hurried into his house and gathered milk, butter, and cheese. Ernesto loaded everything on Ocotillo, his burro, and headed for the market. A few hours later Ernesto returned with enough tanned leather to cut one hundred pairs of sandals.

"All of it?" Tessa asked. "You sold *all* the cheese?"

8   (PUEHR koh) *Puerco* means "pig."
9   (MEE hoe) *Mijo* means "my son."

Ernesto nodded. "*Sí.* And all the milk and butter as well." Ernesto laid the leather on the table. "Horacio told me he's planning to kill ten of his cows to make sandals."

Tessa stared at him. "You know how **deceptive** Don Horacio is about money. He's jealous of us, Ernesto. Why would he tell you about this fortune when he's so greedy?"

Tessa helped him cut the leather. "I don't trust Horacio. He's always cheating us. He stole our mustang Encanto."

"He didn't steal the horse, Tessa. He bet me that his horse was better than mine. So we raced—and I lost. He won the horse."

"*¡Cielos!*[10] Haven't you figured it out, Ernesto? He cheated you. I'm sure he's the one who put burrs under Encanto's saddle. He *always* tricks you. And he always wins. This is a trick too. I know it."

When the sandals were ready, Tessa packed some *tacos, frijoles,*[11] and *tortillas.* She filled three **gourds** with water. Then she helped Ernesto pack the sandals onto the burro.

Ernesto smiled. "It's not far, Tessa. Don't worry. And when I return, we'll be rich."

Tessa pulled her *rebozo* over her long, straight hair. "Be careful. There are bandits in those mountains."

The New Mexico sun burned down on Ernesto and his burro as they followed an old trail leading to the mountains. Ernesto heard the sound of wings. He squinted at the intense sparkle of blue sky. A golden eagle soared overhead.

"Look, Ocotillo. If only we could sprout wings and fly to the mountains with the cool wind in our faces." He sighed. "Oh well, soon we'll be rich. And you won't have to carry burdens for me any more, *amigo.*"[12]

Ernesto gave his faithful burro a long, cool drink. Then, shaded only by wisps of clouds and the shadows of giant *saguaro*[13] cacti, he pushed on toward the mountains.

---

10   (see EH lohs) *Cielos* is an exclamatory word that means "good heavens."

11   (free HOH lehs) *Frijoles* are beans.

12   (ah MEE goh) A*migo* means "friend."

13   (sah GWAH roh) A *saguaro* is a type of cactus that grows in the Southwest.

Early the next day, the people of the mountain village heard someone call "Sandals! Sandals—only ten *pesos* a pair!"

"Is he *loco?*"[14] the people asked one another.

Ernesto explained that his *compadre,* Horacio, told him the people in the mountains needed sandals and were paying ten *pesos* for a single pair.

"*Amigo,*" began one man, "Horacio made a fool of you. The sandals won't sell here because this land is too rocky."

"*¡Santitos!* What shall I do? Where shall I go?"

Another man stepped forward. "Here—take these *pesos* and buy something to eat."

Ernesto stared at the two *pesos.* "If I start soon, I'll be home before dusk."

"Take this lamp, *amigo,*" offered another, "in case you don't get home by nightfall."

Ernesto thanked the people and led his burro away. He was overcome with sadness and shame. "There won't be new dresses for Tessa and my little one. And there won't be a mustang for me. I'm such a fool, Ocotillo. What will I tell Tessa? She'll be angry. She will never forgive me."

Ocotillo brayed. He brayed long and loud.

"I know you're tired and maybe a little angry too." Ernesto patted the burro's neck. "I'll buy you a nice meal, Ocotillo, and then we'll go home. You'll sleep in the barnyard tonight, my friend. I promise."

Later, Ernesto led his burro down the mountain. Clouds covered the sun, and the air turned cold. Rain came fast and hard. "We'll be soaked to the skin, Ocotillo, unless we find shelter."

"Look—a cave." He led the burro inside the mouth of the cave and tied him to a rock. "Stay here, my friend, while I look around."

Ernesto lit the wick of the lamp, tucked the matches into a pocket, and walked deeper into the cave. He held the lantern ahead of him as he stepped into a dreamlike world of icicle-shaped rocks hanging from the ceiling. He wandered along a wide passage and under a stone archway. Where the ceiling

---

14   (LOH koh) *Loco* means "crazy."

sloped, Ernesto stared at long, thick folds of stones that looked like draperies.

The path was so slippery that Ernesto couldn't keep his balance. He reached for the rock ledge to his right and tried to hold on, but lost his grasp and fell. The lamp hit the floor and slid down between two rocks.

"¡*Santitos!* Such a cold, dark place." He heard the echo of his voice, and icy chills rippled through his body.

From deep in the cave came the sound of dripping water. Then came a hollow silence. Ernesto took in a breath and heard his sigh echo long and lonely into the darkness.

He reached down between the cracks for his lamp but could not find it. He continued to search underneath the rocks where a small pool of water formed. As he **groped** around in the sandy soil, he felt something strange; a large round object.

Ernesto ran his hands over the object. A leather bag. He lifted the bag and slowly felt his way back to the mouth of the cave.

"Gold!" He let the glittering coins that filled the bag fall through his fingers. "Real gold!" Ernesto gathered the bag of gold and hurried back to the cave's entrance.

The storm was over, and a sapphire sky reached down to him. Ernesto closed his eyes and felt the wind on his face. He heard the sounds of wind sweeping around the rugged, towering cliffs and through the **craggy** canyons. His burro **nuzzled** against him.

"Ocotillo, my faithful friend." He hugged his burro. "We're rich, *amigo.* Rich." He gave Ocotillo food and some cool water. After he ate and rested for a while, he led his burro down the mountain and into the desert. Just as the first star shone out of an **amethyst** sky, Ernesto and Ocotillo were home.

Tessa and his daughter greeted him. After a meal of *tamales,* corn, and *tortillas,* Ernesto gathered his family around him. "Look—let me show you what I brought for you." He gave his little daughter chocolate and a necklace. And for Tessa, a fine *rebozo* and dress.

"Where are the sandals?" Tessa asked. "Did you sell all of them?"

"No. They're outside, in the barn. We don't need them."

"We're poorer than poor," Tessa cried. "Oh, what are we going to do?"

"Wait, Tessa. Everything's fine." He sat on the floor, opened the bag, and poured out the gold coins.

Tessa dropped to her knees. "*¡Cielos!* You've robbed someone. I'm living with a thief."

Ernesto stared at her for a moment. "*¡Santitos!* How could you think such a thing? I found the gold in a cave. Look at these pouches. They're old. They've been in that cave for who knows how long. Someone hid them and forgot all about them or died long ago."

Tessa caught her breath, covering her mouth with both hands. Then she laughed. "Ernesto—we're rich!"

"*Sí, sí.* We have enough for all our needs—new clothes for you and our little daughter."

Tessa smiled. "And for you, my husband, a mustang. Ten mustangs. You'll have the best corn, tomatoes, and chile peppers in town. And you'll have the finest animals in all of New Mexico."

The next morning, Horacio rode up on the mustang. He rode down the narrow path leading to Ernesto's farm. Tessa stood tall and proud, wearing her new *rebozo* and dress. She stood with her hands on her hips as Horacio rode toward the tender ears of corn and tomatoes, red and ripe, on their curling vines.

Horacio slowed his horse and **dismounted.** He doffed his hat and held it over his heart. "*Buenos días, compadre.*"

Tessa nodded without smiling or speaking.

"I'm happy to see you looking so beautiful. I hear my *compadre* has returned from the mountains."

"*Sí.* He's in the barnyard. See to it you don't crush the vegetables in your haste to see him."

Horacio made no comment. He walked the mustang carefully down the pathway and found Ernesto milking his cow.

"I see you didn't kill your fine, fat cow."

Ernesto stood and patted the cow's glossy side. "*Me, compadre?* How could I? Manzanita means more to me than all the *pesos* in New Mexico."

Horacio looked puzzled. "Then how did you go to the mountains?"

"I sold Manzanita's milk, butter, and cheese and used the money to buy leather to make the sandals."

"And tell me, did you have any luck?"

Ernesto smiled and pulled a handful of gold coins from his pocket. "*Sí, compadre.*"

Horacio blinked and stared.

"But this is nothing, Horacio. Look." Ernesto took another handful of gold coins from his other pocket.

Horacio couldn't speak for a moment. "But—how is this possible?"

"You told me to sell the sandals at ten *pesos* a pair," began Ernesto. "But an old friend from the mountains told me to sell the sandals at twenty *pesos* a pair. Oh, well. That's all water under a cave, so to speak."

Horacio frowned. "Water under a cave?"

"*Sí.* So to speak. Here, *compadre.* Take a coin."

Horacio grabbed all the coins from Ernesto's hand.

Ernesto frowned and looked at the mustang. The horse seemed to plead with dark eyes. "Here, Horatio. Take these coins too." He gave his greedy friend the coins from his other hand. "Only let me have the mustang."

Without so much as a blink, Horacio handed Ernesto the reins and took the gold.

Early the next morning, in the mountain village, the people heard someone call "Sandals! Sandals—only twenty *pesos* a pair!"

"What? Another man selling sandals?" the people asked one another.

"He's *loco.* They're all *loco* in the valley."

"*Sí.* But this man is twice as *loco* as the other."

And in the valley, Ernesto brushed down his mustang and led him out of the barn. He fed the mustang oats and gave him fresh, cool water.

"You're back home where you belong, Encanto. No more whips or spurs, *amigo.* Now you can gallop through the plains and eat all the oats and hay you want."

Ernesto and Tessa became wealthy farmers. But most of their wealth was in their friendships with the poor. They shared their gold with others and became *compadre* and *comadre* to many children over the years.

True to his word, Ernesto was always good to his land and his animals. And for that he was repaid a thousandfold. And more.

INSIGHTS

Many tales exist among Mexican Amercians involving two *compadres,* one rich and one poor. These stories contrast opposite character types and teach a moral lesson about right and wrong.

The rich *compadre* usually pays for his greed, cruelty, jealousy, and selfishness. The poor *compadre* often triumphs, usually because of his generosity, kindness, and devotion to family. In some stories, the poor *compadre* is easily fooled. In other tales, he may be revengeful.

To visitors and natives alike, New Mexico is "The Land of Enchantment." There's a unique beauty found in New Mexico: ancient ruins, spectacular rock formations, sandstone cliffs, and deep purple evening skies and mountains.

Manzanita, the name given to Ernesto's cow, is the name of a shrub that grows in New Mexico. Ocotillo, the name of his burro, is an orange-red flower that blooms in the desert. And his mustang Encanta is named after "The Land of Enchantment."

Caves like the one Ernesto discovers are common in New Mexico. The world's most extraordinary cave is in Carlsbad, New Mexico. One of its chambers, called The Big Room, is 4,000 feet long. More than 13 football fields could fit inside The Big Room, and it is taller than a 20-story skyscraper.

Most caves are damp, dark, and quiet. Water drips from the walls and ceiling. There are often deep streams and underground pools. Caves are darker than a moonless night. In some caves, there is also the sound of wind. The temperature inside caves stays about the same, even though it feels cooler when it's hot outside and warmer on a cold day.

ROMANCE

The Princess of Lake Pátzcuaro

Legend of the Lovers

Love overcomes all obstacles, especially in folktales. Stories of lovers finding each other despite the odds are common in Mexico and the Southwest.

The characters in Mexican American romance tales are often separated by cultural boundaries. In these stories, love not only unites two people, but two cultures as well.

The heroes and heroines in the tales you are about to read are transformed, or changed, by their love. Notice what they discover about themselves as you read.

The Princess of Lake Pátzcuaro

VOCABULARY PREVIEW

The following words appear in the story. Review the list and get to know the words before you read the story.

anguish—great sorrow; agony
alienation—separation; withdrawing
arrogant—boastful; conceited
attendant—servant; a person who waits upon another
brooded—thought about seriously; sulked
dueling—conflicting; opposing
exquisite—beautiful; elaborate
indigo—a deep reddish blue
insensitive—lacking feeling; unkind
intertwined—united by winding together; braided
intrigued—fascinated; captivated
motif—theme; pattern
obsessed—absorbed; fascinated
tranquil—peaceful
wistful—sad; longing

MAIN CHARACTERS

Mintzita—a Princess
Antonio—a Prince
Doña Blanca—beautiful young Spanish woman

The Princess of Lake Pátzcuaro

Inspired by a tale from Mexico

A young princess refuses to adapt to the ways
of the Spanish colonists. Accepting their ways
means rejecting her past.
Can she learn to accept the new and still hold
on to her past?

Long ago there lived a Princess named Mintzita who fell in love with a Prince named Antonio. They lived happily near the beautiful Lake Pátzcuaro.[1] Then it came to pass that Cortés, the Spanish conqueror, found and invaded their fair country, the land of the Purépecha[2] people. The Prince and Princess continued to live in the same region, but their lives changed in many ways.

The Prince quickly won over the Europeans with his intelligence and was made governor of Michoacán.[3] That state was a one-day journey away. He and the Princess moved from their simple Purépecha home into the palatial governor's mansion the Europeans built. He learned the language and traditions of the Spaniards.

But the Princess didn't adapt easily like the Prince. She wasn't used to the extravagance of the Spaniards. She had always been known for her simple elegance. Also, she did not

---

1 (PATS kwah roh) The word *pátzcuaro* means "seat of ancient temples." It is the name of a beautiful lake in Mexico and the name of a town that is famous for its crafts.

2 (Poo REH peh chah) Purépecha is the name given to the native people of the area surrounding lake Pátzcuaro.

3 (Mee zwah KAHN) Michoacán is a state in Mexico that means "place of the fish."

learn to speak Spanish. As a result, she grew quiet among her husband's foreign guests.

With sad eyes, the Princess watched Antonio speak Spanish to the Europeans. He took great interest in the new markets and restaurants that opened in the city. On days when he rode off to enjoy the city with the Spaniards, she worried about him. She was afraid of the horses—horrible beasts—with their thundering hooves and wild eyes. What if one of the beasts threw the Prince—or trampled him?

"I fear for my husband when he is with the Spaniards," she told a friend. "They have strange ways, and I do not trust them. If anything would happen to the Prince, I do not think I could live."

The Prince and Princess were often invited to festivals and dances. Mintzita admired the fabulous gowns worn by the Spanish women. But she worried that one of these beautiful women might someday steal Antonio's heart. The Spanish women gathered around the Prince when he walked into the ballroom. Antonio charmed the women who wanted to talk with him and dance with him.

Mintzita tried to enjoy the festivities, though she didn't feel comfortable in her simple gowns and shawls. She longed to fit in, but she didn't know how. And so she began to dread parties and dances and withdrew more into herself.

"Why do you leave me alone so much?" she asked the Prince one evening. "Why don't you stay here and talk to me?"

Antonio looked up from the book he was reading. "But I'm here now, my lady. I talk to you even when we aren't talking. You soothe my soul with your gentle, quiet ways. I don't like leaving you by yourself, and I miss you whenever I'm away."

Mintzita picked up her embroidery work and stared at the designs. "How I long for our other life. I miss our royal home in Tzintzuntzán,[4] and I dream of Lake Pátzcuaro every night. It's such a **tranquil** place, and I feel at home near its blue waters. I long to see the islands of Lake Pátzcuaro with their flowers and butterflies of every imaginable color."

---

4   (Seen soon SAHN) The city of Tzintzuntzán is the old Tarascan capital.

The Prince's dark eyes looked tired and sad. "We can't go there now, my lady. But I promise we'll go there soon."

Mintzita gazed at him. "Oh, I wish we were going tomorrow, Antonio. I can hear the wind in the trees, and I see the sun sparkle on the smooth lake. When I close my eyes, I'm there. I know I'll dream of the lake and islands tonight."

She smiled at Antonio. "I stay here only because of my love for you."

The Prince sat next to Mintzita and took her hands in his. "I'm sorry you're lonely. I miss our home, too, but as governor I'm expected to work with the Spaniards."

"You work with them, you speak their strange language, you entertain them. Tell me, my Prince, do you like the Spanish ways more than the traditions of the Purépecha people?"

"The Spaniards are here, Mintzita, and I must make the best of it. I do like our new bishop. I deeply appreciate the different handicrafts he has taught our people. These skills freed the Purépecha Indians from a life of misery in the mines."

Mintzita turned away. "Yes, Tata Vasco[5] is a wise and wonderful bishop. I like visiting the sick in the new hospital he founded for our people. 'Princess! Mintzita!' they call to me. Our people always bring joy to my heart.

"Antonio, it's so sad, the way the Spanish mining lords and landowners have treated our people. It was the backbreaking work of the Purépecha people that built the roads for their fancy carriages. I hate those carriages and the noise they make in the streets."

The Prince turned her to face him again. "I know how you feel, my lady. But we're living in a changing world, and I can't bring back the past, though I wish with all my heart that I could."

The Princess sighed. "Oh, Antonio, how can you like the Spaniards? They're such **arrogant, insensitive** people. They keep calling us Tarascans. Don't they know our people are called Purépecha?"

---

5   (TAH tah VAHS koh) Tata Vasco is the affectionate name given to Don Vasco de Quiroga, the first bishop of Michoacán.

"We're part of both worlds now—Tarascan and Purépecha," replied the Prince. "We can never go back, Mintzita. As time passes, you'll get used to the ways of the foreigners."

But time passed, and it did not change Mintzita's feelings. With growing **alienation,** the Princess watched as more Spaniards came to live in Michoacán. The Europeans visited the palace often, and their ways spread further into Michoacán. They introduced not only their language and manners, but also their foods, styles of architecture, and their dancing.

The Prince enjoyed the company of the Spaniards. He was **intrigued** by their ways, especially their dancing. The sophisticated moves and extravagant style contrasted with the simple dances of the Purépecha. One evening in the palace ballroom, he fell under the spell of Doña Blanca,[6] the beautiful but vain daughter of a Spanish nobleman.

Princess Mintzita watched in **anguish** as the young Spanish woman danced in circles around the room. As she danced, the skirt of her luxurious gown shimmered like sunlight on water.

One day while Mintzita was at the marketplace buying clay dishes for the coming palace *fiesta,* she saw Antonio's carriage pass through the stone street and stop. The Prince stepped out of the carriage and waited. A moment later, Doña Blanca walked towards him, and he escorted her to his carriage. Then the two of them rode off together.

The Princess turned away and looked into the eyes of her **attendant.** She tried to smile. "These clay dishes are lovely. I'll buy them for the *fiesta.*"

"Of course, my Princess. They are indeed beautiful."

Mintzita struggled to hold back tears. When she returned to the palace, she stayed alone for the rest of the afternoon. The Princess was devastated—torn between **dueling** emotions. She was so fearful of losing Antonio that she longed to be like the golden-haired woman who stole his heart.

Mintzita hid her feelings from Antonio. She smiled, but her heart was breaking. She said, "Would you like me to read to

---

6   (DOH nyah BLAHN kah) Doña Blanca de Fuenrara was the wealthy daughter of a Spanish nobleman and landholder.

you?" and "I've been so busy preparing for the *fiesta.*" But the words in her heart said, "What will I do if I lose you?" and "Would you love me more if my hair were like the sunlight and my eyes were the color of Lake Pátzcuaro?"

The Prince sat next to the Princess. "I've invited many Spaniards to the *fiesta.*"

"And the beautiful Doña Blanca—have you invited her?" Mintzita wondered. But she said, "I'm looking forward to the *fiesta.*"

"Are you, my lady? You look so sad tonight. I know how lonely you are when I'm away from the palace."

"I'm not lonely anymore," she lied. "I enjoy being with my friends and helping the cooks. I read, I work at my loom, and I enjoy embroidering. I love creating new patterns and designs."

The Prince looked at the butterflies she was embroidering. "Your sewing is the most imaginative I've seen."

The Princess smiled. "Tell me, my Prince, what would you like me to wear at the *fiesta?*"

Antonio looked away. "It makes no difference to me. Choose whatever you wish."

"No difference? He doesn't care," she thought. "His dark eyes are only for Doña Blanca now. Oh, I've lost him."

"Are you crying, my lady?" The Prince stared at her. "What's wrong?"

"Oh, I'm all right. I'm just a little sad, dreaming of Lake Pátzcuaro."

Mintzita couldn't sleep that night. She felt lost and alone. Antonio had loved her once, but that was long ago in a different time and a different place. And now, in her loneliest hours, nothing could bring back those happier times.

On the evening of the *fiesta,* Mintzita wore her prettiest royal gown with embroidery around the neckline, sleeves, and hem. Her waist-long hair was **intertwined** with multicolored ribbons.

She said nothing when Doña Blanca arrived wearing a fabulous ball gown with a bejeweled bodice and lavish layered skirt. She said nothing when Antonio danced with the beautiful

Spanish woman. She said nothing, but her **wistful** eyes seemed to ask, "Would you still care for me if I dressed like Doña Blanca?"

Princess Mintzita watched the beautiful Doña Blanca late into the evening. Finally, when she could take no more, the Princess quietly left the palace. She took nothing with her, and she said nothing to her husband. She knew that she must go to Lake Pátzcuaro.

The Princess began the one-day journey on a narrow path that led into the woods. She wandered for what seemed like hours before she came to the first of three streams. When she came to the water's edge, she dipped her hands and lifted them to splash her face. The water refreshed her, for she made it over a large hill to the second stream in a short time.

Mintzita continued to walk toward the lake, stopping only to rest once more on her journey. When she finally reached the lake, she collapsed in exhaustion and joy. Then, she somehow found the strength to row a fisherman's small boat to La Pacanda Island,[7] a place that she knew well.

There, on the island, the Princess knew she would find happiness. She was at home in the forest and found peace listening to the gentle waves of the lake. Each morning, she woke up to the fragrance of flowers that covered the island.

Mintzita's life was simple now. She gathered nuts and berries from a forested area and caught fish off the rocky shore. In the morning, she often washed her clothes in the lake and dried them on the branches of trees. The peacefulness of the island contrasted strikingly with the noise and disruptions of the governor's mansion. In this peacefulness, the Princess turned to weaving. She wove a beautiful blanket using the timeless stepped-fret **motif** of the Purépecha.

One evening when a pale, full moon rose into the twilight, Mintzita stood by the shore of the island. She looked at the moon and smiled. "Here I am, dear Mother Moon. I've come back to my cascading falls and sheltering forest. I'm happy here

---

7   (Lah Pah KAHN dah) La Pacanda Island is one of three islands in Lake Pátzcuaro. The island is know for its abundant flowers.

with the creatures of my youth, and now I'll grow strong again. Tell me how to win back Antonio's heart."

Meanwhile, back at the palace, Antonio grew deeply worried about the Princess. When she had disappeared from the *fiesta,* the Prince repeatedly searched the palace and its grounds. He paced up and down the front walkway and waited for her return. Then he withdrew in the mansion and **brooded**, his dark eyes shadowed with worry.

When a week passed and the Princess still hadn't appeared, Antonio began to despair. Everything in the palace reminded him of the Princess—the baskets and handicrafts of the Purépecha people, the painting of Lake Pátzcuaro, the embroidery that decorated the tablecloths. He remembered the sound of her voice and the way she smiled when she spoke to him. He missed the fragrance of her long black hair.

One day the Prince went to his people and asked if they knew where their Princess was hiding.

"She is on Lake Pátzcuaro," a fishermen told him.

"She is on the island of flowers," a Purépecha woman told him.

Some said they saw her sitting at a loom in a hollowed willow tree where she wove exquisite patterns on never-ending cloth that lay in folds all around her.

"She speaks to no one," the Purépecha said.

"She weaves by sunlight and moonlight," the women said.

It was told that when the rains came, Mintzita stood gazing out at the lake, the rain pouring over her.

"She's **obsessed,**" they told the Prince.

"She's mad," the people warned.

But Mintzita wasn't obsessed. And she was not mad. She was happy on the island where hills were starred by flowers the color of amethysts and rubies. The Princess was inspired by the island to create fantastic weavings and embroidery work. And every night, under the stars and with the breeze rippling the water, the Princess talked to her guardian.

"Sweet Mother Moon," said Mintzita, "Here I am. It's your daughter, Mintzita. I am at peace on this island surrounded by your mystical lake. Antonio is near, Mother Moon. I still have work to complete before he finds me."

Antonio had left for Lake Pátzcuaro immediately after he learned that Mintzita was there. A fisherman lent him a boat for crossing the water. He reached La Pacanda Island before dawn. Guided by the brilliance of a morning star, the Prince searched for the Princess until that evening. He found her standing in front of an ancient pyramid.

Antonio stared at Mintzita. She was more beautiful than ever. The Prince had never seen the Princess wearing such magnificent clothes. Her blouse was embroidered with the ancient Purépecha designs of hummingbirds and butterflies. Her *rebozo*[8] was like the nighttime water of Lake Pátzcuaro with white-gold moonbeams dancing on the waves.

Her **indigo** skirt, longer in back than in front, was an abundance of cascading blue pleats that spread along the ground like a huge fan. An apron that seemed spun from the fabric of the moon covered the front of the skirt. And along the hem of the apron, embroidery shimmered and danced in the shadows.

Mintzita's hair was interlaced with ribbons the color of wildflowers.

"Antonio, why don't you speak to me?"

The Prince took a step towards the Princess, then hesitated. "When you left, you took away my life. Why did you leave?"

Mintzita gazed at him. "You abandoned me when a Spanish *doña* stole your heart. I could see that you would eventually become more Spanish than Purépecha. I had to leave. I had to find my own way."

The Prince looked out at the lake. "And you found your way on this lonely island?"

She moved towards him, the long skirt rippling like blue waves. "Mother Moon helped me, Antonio. I asked her to help me hold on to my Purépecha past while I embrace the ways of the Spanish. Then I began to weave this fine gown by blending the embroidery patterns of the Purépecha and the Spanish."

---

8   (reh BOH soh) A *rebozo* is a shawl.

"Yes, my Princess. Your creation reminds me of both the serenity of this lake and the excitement of the city. The gown is part of you and part of our people. I've always loved you not only for your **exquisite** beauty but for your imaginative creations. You are the most beautiful woman in Michoacán."

After spending several days together at Lake Pátzcuaro, the Prince and the Princess returned to Michoacán. From that time on, she no longer hovered quietly in the governor's mansion but took an active part in her husband's affairs. She learned all she could of the Spanish language and culture, and in time she became well-loved throughout the region.

The Princess never forgot the Purépecha. The Prince would not let her. Each year he accompanied her on a journey to Lake Pátzcuaro. When they approached, he would let go of her hand and let her walk to the shore alone. There, she would watch the sparkling water and listen to the gentle waves.

*   *   *

The clothes created by Mintzita during her days alone at Lake Pátzcuaro were copied by the women of Michoacán. The hearts and souls of the Purépecha and the Spaniards were blended and celebrated in the unique designs. Even today, the fiesta dresses of Michoacán are fashioned like Mintzita's timeless creations with rich embroidery, indigo blues, and designs of flowers and moonbeams inspired by Lake Pátzcuaro.

INSIGHTS

This story is based in part on legend and in part on historical events. After the Spanish Conquest of Mexico ended in 1521, the Purépecha capital of Tzintzuntzán was placed under the Spanish crown. But the Indian king still ruled his people as governor.

The last emperor's sons moved to Pátzcuaro. The oldest son became governor but soon died. His younger brother, Don Antonio Huitziméngari y Caltzontzin, became governor. Don Antonio was bright, handsome, and a charming prince. He built his palace near the main square in Pátzcuaro. He loved books and read many of the classics. He built a beautiful, extensive library in his home which is still called the "House of the Governor."

In 1540, the new bishop, Don Vasco de Quiroga, named Pátzcuaro as the new capital city of Michoacán. The bishop then founded the hospital of Santa Fe to serve as the center of religion and politics as well as to care for the sick. He gathered the Indians into communities and established rules to govern their daily lives.

The Spaniards brought the old world to Mexico and imposed many of their ways on the native people. But the Purépechas kept their own traditions whenever possible. The result was a blending of cultures with many legends and folktales reflecting both peoples.

Although many customs were destroyed, Purépecha family life remains unchanged. The people still have two occupations—agriculture and one chosen trade such as metal work, ceramics, weaving, leather work, or woodworking. The Purépecha are expert metal workers in gold, silver, and copper.

In Mexican American tales of romance, the hero and heroine are often separated by cultural obstacles. In this story, the heroine struggles to accept Spanish cultural influences. In other tales, the lovers are separated by different tribal upbringings. Typically, one of the characters must undergo a transformation before the two can be united.

Legend of the Lovers

VOCABULARY PREVIEW

The following words appear in the story. Review the list and get to know the words before you read the story.

acrid—sharp; harsh
alliance—union; association
belittled—humiliated; discredited
cascaded—poured; rushed in
conspired—plotted; schemed
decreed—ordered
flank—the right or left side of an army
hallucinating—having visions; imagining
inferior—low in position or rank; second-rate
jubilation—joy; celebration
prodigious—vast; huge
rendezvous—meeting; encounter
resigned—calm; submissive
revive—renew; restore
subsided—let up; grew less
trance—daze; dreamlike state
treachery—falseness; deceit

MAIN CHARACTERS

Izta—an Aztec Princess
Popo—a warrior who belongs to the Chichimeca, a wandering tribe of hunters

Legend of the Lovers

Adapted from a tale from Mexico

*Travelers to Mexico often comment on the
beauty and majesty of the two mountains
known as Popocatépetl and Iztaccíhuatl. But
few know the legend of their origin.*

Princess Izta[1] had been ill for weeks and now she lapsed into a coma. Prince Popo[2] felt as if his heart would break.

"You must awaken," the Prince said as he sat by Izta's side and brooded. "My love, since our banishment, we've faced many difficulties. We've endured a long period of isolation and near starvation. Just as we've overcome these problems, so will you overcome this illness."

He bent down and spoke softly. "If only I had the power to heal you. I would give anything, do anything, if it would make you well again."

At that moment he began to cry, fearing that soon she would die. When his sobbing **subsided,** he wiped away the tears. Then he softly kissed his wife's face, admiring each delicate feature.

As the Prince knelt by his wife's bed, a deep voice filled the room. "Fear not, my son," rumbled the voice. "The gods have seen your suffering, and they have taken pity on you."

"Who are you?" stammered the Prince.

"I am the god of the mountain."

---

1   (EES tah) Izta is short for Iztaccíhuatl, an Aztec name that means "woman of the snows."

2   (PO po) Popo is short for Popocatépetl.

"What do you want?" asked the Prince. "The story of your love has reached the heavens and touched the hearts of the gods," said the voice. "Your Princess will awaken soon. Tell her that we have granted you this night together."

"What will happen after tonight?" asked the Prince.

"All your questions will be answered with the dawn," came the god's reply. Then there was silence.

The Prince couldn't believe what he heard. He thought he must be **hallucinating.** Perhaps his grief drove him insane.

But then, as the god had promised, Izta began to awaken. Her fingers moved, and her eyes opened. She smiled and sat up and with a look of concern asked, "Why do you look so sad, my husband?"

"You have been very ill, my beloved. I thought you would die. But the gods have granted us one more night together." He took her by the hand.

The Princess slowly stood up and looked around her. She gazed up to the surrounding hills and then looked down at the stream. "Are we still in the valley?"

"Yes. We're still in the *calli*[3] I built when we first arrived."

"This valley seems to stand still," the Princess said. "Nothing has changed since we were first banished by my father."

"Yes, the valley has stayed the same," said the Prince as he gazed out over the scene, "just like my love for you."

The Princess smiled at him. "I feel the same, my husband," she said softly. "Our love is the center of my life."

"Do you remember the first time we saw each other?" asked the Prince.

"I'll never forget that day," smiled the Princess. After a moment's thought she smiled slyly. "And did you know I arranged that meeting?"

"No!" replied the Prince.

"It all started when my father declared that I marry. He told me that I could choose whomever I wished as long as he was an Aztec noble."

"Tell me more," said the Prince.

---

3   (KAH lee) A *calli* is a house.

"Several months passed before I complained to him. 'Father,' I said, 'these young Aztec nobles are spoiled. They are as immature as green corn.'

"But my father demanded that I marry within my race. It was Aztec law and I had to obey.

"At that time, it was rumored that a Chichimeca[4] Prince was to visit a nearby marketplace on the island-city of Tenochtitlán.[5] I heard many stories about this Prince. Some said he was extraordinarily handsome."

"That would be me, right?" asked the Prince with a mischievous grin.

"Quiet," demanded the Princess. She put her finger on his lips. "This is my part of the story. You'll have your turn soon enough.

"One day," continued the Princess, "I asked my maids about the Prince. You see, they went to the market every day, and I knew they would be able to repeat all the gossip. 'No, not a Chichimeca!' one told me, horrified. 'Chichimecas look like dogs. Everyone calls them "Dog People." '

'They're barbarians,' another said. 'They eat the raw meat of rabbits and live in mountain caves like hordes of bats. For their clothing they wear dirty animal skins.'

"You should have seen how my ladies of the palace fluttered about," Izta continued.

"Despite their words, I was curious to see this 'Dog Prince.' So I set up a plan to meet him."

Izta paused in her story as a gust of wind blew under the cloth that covered the doorway of the *calli*. She shivered.

"Please continue your story," urged the Prince as he placed a blanket over her shoulders.

"One morning," she said, nestling into the blanket, "I called for my litter.[6] I had the bearers carry me to the marketplace. I knew that the streets of the marketplace were too narrow for two

---

4   (Chee chee MEH kah) Chichimeca is the name of a wandering tribe of sturdy hunters and bowmen.

5   (Teh noch tee T'LAN) Tenochtitlán is the capital city of the Aztec empire.

6   A litter is a covered and curtained couch provided with shafts. It is used to carry passengers.

litters to pass at the same time," she added. "I decided to wait until you came.

"Suddenly, there you were. I remember it so well. The gold and jewels on your litter shone in the sun. You sat so proud, dressed in a handsome *tilmantli*[7] embroidered with the dog-totem design of the Chichimeca. It was not the dirty animal skin I had been warned about.

"Your face was framed by long hair, and you wore a crown of feathers. My maids kept making the most unusual faces, and their hand signals were as wild as frightened monkeys. They wanted me to lower the curtain to my litter. However, I couldn't move. I just sat staring at you until you looked up and saw me.

"Not only did the 'Dog Prince' of Chichimeca allow me to pass, but you went out of your way to be polite. You got out of your litter, bowed low, and gestured for us to pass."

Izta took her husband's hand. "The rest of the day went by as if in a daze. My attendants were desperately trying to get my attention. 'Izta! My lady!' they called. 'We must leave quickly. You're as red as a *tomatl!*'[8] They thought I was sick, for they had rarely seen me blush. Indeed, I was sick, but not in the way that they thought."

"I was swept up in a **trance** of my own," replied the Prince with a laugh. He warmed his hands over the fire. "My heart soared as high as a thunderbird. I thought your face looked like that of a beautiful goddess. The sun made your white tunic glow.

"My aide tried to get my attention," continued the Prince. "'Dear Prince, are you all right?' my aide asked. 'It was that girl, wasn't it?' I hardly heard him. 'She is like a white bird in the sky,' I murmured. 'I must meet her. I must win her for my own.'

"My aide was horrified. 'It is against the law for you, a Chichimeca, to so much as look at an Aztec princess. You can never marry her, Highness. Her laws forbid it.'

---

7   (teel MAHN t'lee) A *tilmantli* is a cloak that is knotted on one shoulder.

8   (toh MAH t'l) *Tomatl* is the Aztec word for tomato.

"His words buzzed in my ear like a fly. I paid no attention to him or anything else. My zest for bargaining in the marketplace vanished.

"I continued to dream even as we passed through the narrow pathways lined with merchants. We passed barber shops, game birds, medicinal herb sellers, and clothing. But none interested me. Even the elaborate featherwork didn't keep me from daydreaming.

"'My Prince, you always comment on the skillful featherwork from Pátzcuaro,'[9] my aide reminded me. And when a parrot squawked, my aide said, 'Even this bird is trying to wake you up to your senses, my lord.'

"Later my assistant tried to interest me in some food. He unraveled steamy corn husks and commented on the aroma of the thick corn crust and yellow chili. But I declined because I had a strange loss of appetite.

"On the return trip home, I pondered whether or not I should follow my yearnings. I decided to hike up the winding trails that led south to the mountains of Ajusco.[10]

"I began to feel angry at the rigid laws that divided the Aztec and the Chichimeca. On the long trek back to my mountain home I became **resigned.** I told myself, 'Forget the White Lady, the beautiful princess of Tenochtitlán.'"

"I struggled with the same problem," added Izta. "I no longer cared about anything. I was miserable. I moped around the palace as if my best friend had died.

"My father thought the wondrous gardens of Xochimilco[11] would bring back the happy daughter he remembered. So he made preparations for me to go south. On the day of my departure, he warned me sternly, 'No stopping to talk to any foreign nobles.'

" 'Yes, Father,' I promised. Then I bowed and respectfully stepped away.

---

9   (PAHTS kwah roh) Pátzcuaro is a town on the shore of a beautiful lake west of Mexico City.

10   (Ah WHOS koh) Ajusco is a city about twelve miles southwest of Mexico City.

11   (Soh chee MEEL koh) Xochimilco is an area south of Tenochtitlán known for the cultivation of flowers.

"However, I had a plan," said Izta. "I quickly went about making preparations for the trip. Then I swore my maids to secrecy."

The Prince poured some hot tea into a cup and handed it to Izta. "Here, warm yourself with this."

"I love the aroma," Izta said. "It's so good on a winter night like this. Tell me about our **rendezvous** at Xochimilco. I know our story well, my love. But tell me your part once again."

"When I received your invitation," Prince Popo began, "I knew nothing could stop me from seeing you. I retraced my way north and found you right away. Your white dress was embroidered with flower designs. A garland of dahlia adorned your lustrous black hair. But when I approached, your litter bearers sprang up and carried you away," the Prince laughed.

"You leaned out of your litter and called, 'As long as I don't stop, I'm following my father's wishes. He's forbidden me to stop and speak to any foreign noble.'"

"Later, we walked along the edge of the water," the Princess recalled. "We made sure we kept moving."

"Then we floated along the canal in two flower-decorated barges," he said. "Your boat floating alongside mine.

"And while your ladies-in-waiting were nodding off to sleep," he continued. "We talked about everything—childhood memories, our parents, and the ways of our people."

"I came to discover the history of your people," Izta added. "I never knew that the Chichimecas were cousins to the Aztecs and that long ago my people were the last to leave the region of the caves.

"I learned that the Poet-King[12] had been a Chichimeca," she added. "Recite some of his verses for me, my husband, while I prepare something to eat."

Popo helped Izta place the *cumal*[13] on the stones. He sliced a prickly pear as Izta prepared the corn dough for the tortillas.

---

12   The Poet-King, also known as Netzahuaslcoyotl, was a Texcoco ruler of Chichimeca origin who reigned from 1424 to 1460 A.D.

13   (KOO mahl) A *cumal* is a flat clay disk used for cooking.

As they worked, the Prince quoted some of the old ruler's poetry by heart.

> Tell me, is it true?
> One lives on Earth
> But for a little while?
> If it be of fine gold, it be crunched
> Be it of precious jade, it be broken
> Of quetzal[14] feathers, it will fade
> All shall not last
> No thing shall be forever
> All lives on Earth
> But for a little while.

"Yes, life is short, my love," Izta said. "And here we are spending our time talking—just as we did that first night in the garden."

"There's so much to talk about, my love. If your father had his way, we wouldn't talk at all," said the Prince.

"I know," said the Princess.

"I remember the first time I sent a message to your father," continued Popo. "I told him of my love for you and asked his permission to marry you."

"My father was furious," the Princess responded. "I had never seen him so angry. 'You have brought shame to me,' he raged. 'How could you even consider marrying someone so unworthy, so **inferior**?'

"'I love Popo,' I told him. 'We could learn much from his people. I won't marry any other,' I said. But he only grew angrier. At last, he said, 'For your disobedience, you will be confined to your apartments.'"

"Fortunately," said the Prince as he looked into the Princess' eyes, "a kind guard allowed us to meet secretly.

"About that time," he went on, "I received a letter from your father. I didn't know what to think when, in the letter, he offered you in marriage. He then asked if in exchange the Chichimecas

---

14   (KEHT sahl) A *quetzal* is a bird from Mexico that is considered one of the most beautiful in the world.

would help the Aztecs in war. My aide warned me, 'Do not involve yourself in this plan! Don't you remember the cowardly deed even our own Poet-King committed?'

"I remembered that a much beloved Chichimeca ruler had **conspired** to send one of his warriors into battle. When the warrior was killed, the cruel monarch was free to take the man's wife. I asked myself, 'Am I being set up to be killed in battle?'

"I decided that I must take a chance and accept your father's offer. I could only hope that he was serious about an **alliance** between the Aztecs and the Chichimecas.

"I soon arrived at Tenochtitlán with many warriors. A great battle was fought. My troops held one **flank**. But soon your father's true purpose became known. The Aztec generals withdrew their armies and left us to fight alone. They thought, no doubt, that we would quickly be defeated.

"However, the generals underestimated the Chichimecas' fighting skills. Combat was long and fierce. But I led the final charge and pushed our foes beyond the mountains.

"There were many casualties. With battered shield, broken obsidian lance, and club, we were disheartened by the **treachery** of the Aztecs.

"My aide tried to **revive** my spirit. 'We must celebrate our victory and honor those who have fallen. And let's not forget your coming wedding,' he exclaimed. When the other men heard his words, they began to gather around me. In Chichimeca fashion, the men danced in a circle and cried out as they shot their arrows into the sky in celebration.

"But our **jubilation** was cut short," continued Prince Popo. "Your father sent word that you had fallen ill and died."

"At the same time," the Princess joined in, "my father deceived me by telling me that you were killed in the battle."

The Prince looked down in sadness. "I had to return to Tenochtitlán to see for myself. It wasn't until I arrived at the palace and found you in the garden that I knew you were alive. I rushed into the garden to see you. I could not wait to hold you once again."

The Princess reached out to touch the Prince's hand. "My father gave us no other choice but to leave. He shouldn't have been surprised that we ran away to be married. He drove us away."

"Yes," said the Prince, who looked off into the distance. "It was he who rejected us, even when we returned and announced our marriage. He **belittled** me in front of the court. He said, 'You'll never be a part of this family. Either you will undo what you have done, or both of you shall be banished.'"

"No one should be given such a choice," the Princess added. "We could not undo our marriage, and yet we dreaded banishment.

"My love, when we fled," the Princess continued, "I believed we would be free to return shortly. I thought my father would come to accept you."

"He never did," the Prince said as he looked down. "That is why we have remained outcasts and had no choice but to wander through the Valley of the Lakes."

The Princess thought back to the first difficult year. "We were near starvation when we finally settled in this valley. Life seemed to improve though. You hunted in the forest and cleared trees for planting."

"Yes. Things improved, but your father never took back his order of banishment."

Just then, the faint light of dawn began to fill the room. Izta began to weaken.

"I'm so tired," she said as she leaned back into her bed. "What will happen to us?"

"I'm not sure," replied the Prince. "The god promised we would be honored—but I don't know how."

Izta looked up at her husband and held his hand. "We have been happy," she said softly. The Prince held her hand and watched the torch burn out into a swirl of smoke.

The Prince remembered the words of the mountain god: "You must say your farewells by dawn, for we have **decreed** that both of you will fall into a great slumber."

At that moment, the Prince heard the mountain god speak, "It is time."

"What am I to do?" asked the Prince.

"Carry your beloved in your arms. Walk to the west. Soon you shall partake in a great creation."

The Warrior Prince cradled his lovely Princess in his arms. The small copper bells in Izta's hem rang softly in the cool morning breeze as he carried her. He walked all that day and night without rest and without tears up the path to the mountains.

After the Prince reached the western slope, he heard a mighty rumble. He felt the earth tremble, then shake with a violent fury. He saw a row of hills explode with such force that an entire forest of pines was leveled to the ground.

Huge clouds of ash spread up and out until they filled the sky. The great dark clouds glowed red from the heat of the lava. The Prince smelled the **acrid** fumes of sulfur in the air. He feared he might not complete his task.

Bolts of lightning zigzagged from the newly-formed craters. He saw the jagged lines of lightning flash through the clouds. The erupting volcanoes spewed rivers of molten lava.

Then the gods joined their **prodigious** powers to put out the eruptions. A great snowfall stormed over the volcanoes. From the heart of the volcano, he heard the mountain god speak, "Carry your Princess to the top of the northern mountain. Take her to the resting place we have prepared for her."

Prince Popo did as he was told. When he reached the resting place, he lowered Izta onto a mound of fragrant white flowers. A flat rock became her headrest; her fine long hair **cascaded** over the edge.

"You will find peace here, my lady," he told her. She moaned softly as if she understood. "The gods promised to keep us together."

He sat faithfully by her side. The outline of Izta's form resembled the jagged stone along the top of the mountain. The sculpted rock was that of a woman in repose.

"Take up your lance and shield," said the god. "You have one more task. Go to the higher peak of the other mountain. The glowing crater will become a great torch whose light will keep vigil over the 'Sleeping Princess of the Snows.' From this day forward an ever-present snow will shelter the two of you as you sleep."

The Prince held the sacred lance and shield. The lance was decorated with precious stones, and the shield was covered with the finest featherwork he had ever seen.

As he prepared to leave, he spoke one last time to his beloved. "The people of this great valley will tell our story," the Prince said. "And when this mountain rumbles and I send out plumes of smoke, they will all know that I am mourning for you, my Princess."

Gentle snows fell on the Prince and Princess. In a gesture of power and love, the gods transformed the couple into magnificent mountains. The gods gave the spirit of each lover its own majestic mountain home.

The snow-covered mountains, side by side, became Mexico's noble reminder of a great eternal love.

INSIGHTS

"Legend of the Lovers" has been told for many generations to explain the creation of the twin volcanoes in Mexico. In the oldest version of the story, the offspring of two gods become young lovers. The couple disobeys the gods by meeting secretly, and as their punishment, they are transformed into two volcanoes.

In later retellings, humans replace the disobedient gods. The story takes on characteristics found in *Romeo and Juliet.* For instance, the young lovers come from different tribal groups. This part of the story is believed to be adapted from the Toltecs, a group of people that dominated central and southern Mexico prior to the Aztecs. According to legend, a Toltec Princess took the forbidden step of marrying a Chichimecan Prince.

Many countries have stories about a prince who comes to awaken a sleeping princess. It was a familiar legend among the ancient kingdoms of Egypt and Greece and the early peoples of England. However, the Aztecs introduced a unique element—a coming invasion. According to the story, someday the Prince would awaken his Princess and cast out foreign invaders.

After the Spanish conquered the Aztecs in 1521, the story of Izta and Popo took on greater significance. People believed that the Golden Age of the Montezuma Kings would return to power once the volcanoes cast out the Spaniards. People of Tenochtitlán began to worship the two volcanoes. Offerings of food, ears of corn, and copal incense were placed by the mountains. People made token images of "Popo" and "Izta" of corn-and-seed dough and placed paper crowns on their heads. Popo's face was given eyes and a mouth.

It seems natural that a rich tradition of storytelling would develop around the two volcanoes. The mountains loom over the landscape of Mexico. The volcanoes reign over the horizon in three Mexican states—Puebla, Cuernavaca, and Morelos. Mount Popocatépetl is 17,976 feet high while Mount Iztaccíhuatl is slightly lower at 17,203 feet.

"Popo" is an active volcano while "Izta" is actually a group of dormant volcanoes. From a distance, one can see the outline of Izta's hair, head, and torso. Both mountains are always capped with snow because of their high altitude.

Throughout Mexico and the Southwest, beautiful illustrations of this story are displayed in homes and sometimes seen in restaurants or bakery shops.